They all got a campus map with their welcome package, and most studied it, looking for secret signs to their future.

You are here, walking up a path at dusk with people you don't know yet.

Up that dotted line, in Building X, you will learn something that will change your life.

Where that red dot is you will be kissed.

There, in that blank space near Location 3, you will break someone's heart.

At Location 7 you will get sick after a hard practice. At 9 you will get sick from huffing.

You will be humiliated on the third floor of Building Y.

And there, in that black clearing, you will find yourself.

THE UPPER CLASS

A NOVEL

HOBSON BROWN, TAYLOR MATERNE & CAROLINE SAYS

HarperTeen
An Imprint of HarperCollins*Publishers*

HarperTeen is an imprint of
HarperCollins Publishers.

The Upper Class

www.harperteen.com

Library of Congress Catalog Card Number: 2006934354
ISBN-10: 0-06-085082-5–ISBN-13: 978-0-06-085082-1

Typography by Jennifer Heuer
❖
First HarperTeen edition, 2007

DEDICATION TK

1

Outside the black window of the country club, moonlight glazes tiger lilies, dripping off the petals like cream. The Connecticut night pants. Tomorrow's forecast is 99 degrees.

Laine Hunt is Going Away. With enormous and untelling blue eyes, she surveys the dining room in its seersucker and gingham glory, trying to know what she's leaving, what exactly she's Going Away from. She's known this room, these portraits of men in banana cashmere sweaters or madras sportcoats, this muted chandelier, since before she knew what knowing was. But the essence of it all slides through her fingers now.

Her mother, Polly, thinks Laine needs cheering up. "It's going to be Parents' Weekend before you even *know* it, sweetie."

That's nice except I don't think I want *it to be Parents' Weekend.* "You're right, Mom. It's not so far away."

Philip Breck, her stepdad, pats his mouth with a linen napkin. "Laine, you'll be back in this room for Christmas before you can blink an eye."

When I get out of this tiny town and our tangled-up house, I'm not exactly going to be racing back.

Everyone speaks lines as though Ang Lee and crew are hiding behind the swinging kitchen doors. Laine envisions rolled-up, much used scripts instead of napkins by each of her family member's plates.

The Brecks look wholesome in dinner table formation: Polly and Philip wear formal and benevolent clubhouse expressions, and Christine and Maggie, Laine's younger sisters, squabble in hushed sibling code over cherries in their Shirley Temples. The two little girls are angelic and glum, nut brown skin covered in Band-Aids and bruises, the diminishing season of sailing and swimming and diving having written its script on their bodies. Like Laine, their hair is white as swan feathers, whiter still against teak skin. Everyone wears lobster bibs, but Laine now sees the flesh out of the red exoskeleton as too surreal to eat, when once it was her favorite food. She dangles the rubbery meat, crudded with white paste, in her butter. And the red sugary drink is disgusting and odd as well. That's how this last year has been: everything normal morphing into strange.

"Good luck!" a friend of Christine's calls to Laine across the room.

Laine thanks her, ducking her head, hating attention called to her family. *My second family.* Philip and his family used to sit over there, Polly and the girls and Thomas over here, when Thomas was still her husband and their father. Now a pink neon sign blinks: *Second Marriage!* over this table, casting a rosy sheen on her sisters' cheekbones. Not like the clubhouse isn't full to bursting with third and fourth and fifth marriages, *but it shouldn't have been my family.*

If this weren't enough, Laine is also worried about a blur of turquoise Izod shirt outside the window, careening about club grounds. Hunter and his crew probably bribed kitchen staff for whipped cream canisters. All summer he's courted Laine—who freezes when she hears his voice, as she does when any guy approaches, so they haven't even kissed, and he's fed up.

A woman who golfs with Polly approaches the table and stage-whispers: "Is she R-E-A-D-Y?"

"Yes, she can barely wait," Polly answers proudly.

The woman looks to Laine. "Are you ready, dear? Ready for lift off?" She makes an awkwardly funny imitation of a rocket with her hands, and everyone kindly laughs at her little joke, wincing simultaneously at her martini breath, strong as gasoline.

"I'm definitely ready," Laine says, craning her neck to see out the window. "I'm really excited."

"I bet you are." The woman winks. "St. Paul's is a fabulous school. My brothers all went there, *way* back in the day."

Polly smiles, indicating that St. Paul's would be great but this is greater: "Laine's going up to Wellington, actually."

"AH!" the woman says, clutching her heart as though Laine had won the Nobel prize, even though she thinks no differently of St. Paul's than of Wellington. "Even *more* fabulous. That lake, my oh my, what a *gorgeous* little corner of the world. And you'll be on the soccer team, no?"

"Field hockey," Philip says.

The woman lets out an extravagant sound, between laughter and self-reproach, then smiles devilishly at Laine, pauses for effect, and says quietly: "I get things mixed up, dear. But one thing I know for darn sure, you are going to have *the greatest experience.*"

The Brecks let that hang in the air, as if Laine had been ordained by a priest. The woman waddles away, clutching her beads, oblivious of white cat hairs stuck to her rump, which is sealed in black slacks and cruelly cinched with a kelly green lizard belt.

And this is what I could become if I stuck around. The woman's name is in the next room, in gilded letters on the tennis plaque, from when she was my age. She probably fell in love with the first guy she kissed, married the first guy she had sex with, got pregnant the first time she tried. She raised her family in the house where she grew up. She drinks the same way her dad drinks, smokes as much as her mom did. And now her intellect is gelatinous (She reads Danielle Steel and Dean Koontz) and her conscience provincial (She donates thousands to museums and still calls the Ecuadorian guys who mow her lawn *boys*).

After dinner, on their way to the door, the Breck family duly stops to talk with the Townes, the Walden-Thornes, the Crandalls. Everyone knows someone who went to Wellington: *J.J. Emerson had a grand old time on the sailing team, Esther Woodbury went from there to Harvard, and didn't Jonas Baker, oh, that's right, he didn't make it through, did he? Ended up at, oh never mind.* James Hill claps Philip on the shoulder and congratulates Laine—his way of communicating: *You're a good man, Phil, to pony up big tuition for a relatively new stepdaughter.*

Outside, under the hot domed sky, Hunter and his buddy materialize out of the dark, swaying like cobras. Up close, Laine can see that Hunter's turquoise shirt is wet with beer. "Ya know, Laine, you coulda called to say good-bye, we shoulda hung out tonight." A green bottle sticks out of his pocket.

"Sorry," Laine mumbles, even though she's not. *Please*

please please go away.

"Are you just too good for everyone?"

Hunter's friend seconds that under his breath and turns away.

Polly clears her throat. Mr. Breck says, *"Hunter"* in a way that says everything.

"I-I'm sorry," Hunter stutters as if just realizing he said that aloud. He backs away. At the Round Hill Country Club in Greenwich, this incident is equivalent to a gun-fight. The Brecks get into the Mercedes, mortified, trembling. Laine is speechless in the backseat, sandwiched between sisters. When once she might have talked back, her way of dealing with conflict has evolved lately into stewing. *What did I do? I never even asked for his attention.*

Laine is accidentally elegant, and has the charm some girls just have without trying, or *because* they don't try. She'll wear a guy's white tennis shirt with a green beach towel around her waist, tops of feet brown and soles pale, picking her way across a gravel drive, and she'll be so simply, quietly, strangely beautiful that boys stare, and men—husbands and dads—look away.

A line of guys, Hunter most recently, has fixated on her, or an idea of her. A hawk picking up the blur of prey on dark ground, not knowing its identity but instinctively, primitively wanting it. Laine is a novice at small talk with guys, heart kicking at the word "hello," and sexually she's a complete rookie. Each guy is disappointed, in order, and then they hate her. *This is one more thing I don't mind leaving behind.*

The car now passes the ghostly house at 203 Round Hill Road. It's tucked behind inky dark bushes overgrown like an ungroomed mustache. Her childhood house, the pre-divorce world, and its lights are off. She already left this house three years ago, but it feels as if tonight, without even having been inside, *that I'm leaving it for good.*

And abandoning the infinite day that existed when they lived there: a ball of sun, the pollen of privet hedges and their tiny flowers gilding the town with perfume, a smear of Coppertone, misty locker rooms at the club, lessons spent baking on the clay fields, sunk in sunny lethargy, then startled by a fast serve. It was one taste: a snack-bar grilled cheese sandwich, lemonade in Styrofoam cups, Italian ices that turned tongues red or blue or green. Laine always flipped her ice to eat the gooey crystals at the bottom first. It was one party: gardenias in buttonholes and gin-and-tonics and tiki torches. It was one night: the three sisters in neon Lily Pulitzer under a fiery moonrise. It was even one face, the face of the community, a composite of concerned and affectionate and freckled and tan and handsome and aristocratic and wise and wrinkled features. It was her upbringing.

Laine lies in bed, knowing she won't sleep in it for months.

Moonlight cuts a sliver in the chintz curtain, spills like milk on the wood floor.

She's slept in many beds, in her family's houses and summerhouses and ski houses. As a guest in other families' houses and pool houses and apartments and villas. At summer camps and field hockey camps and tennis camps. In hotels and on yachts and in tents.

And it doesn't seem to matter what lies outside any of the windows of any of the rooms in which she sleeps. It can be jasmine blooming in the Mediterranean night. It can be Hyde Park lit by street lamps, the hotel room cozy against that London damp. When they stay at Little Nell's in Aspen, a starlit gondola stands only feet away, and a peak shimmers in the distance.

It doesn't matter if it's a room she knows or a room she doesn't, a bed in which she's slept before or where she's never slept, because when she closes her eyes, it's the same nothing inside her eyelids. She falls into the nothing now, into the dreamless hole of her sleep. *Good night,* she thinks to no one.

Hot dawn. Blue mist rolling over lawns, crickets chirping. The molding of Tudor houses wet with heat. The sky simmers, gearing up for another late-summer day.

Laine has left her bike lying in the grass, wipes sweat off her forehead from the twenty-minute ride. When she picks it up later, a silhouette of dew will form the shape of the bicycle, the rest of the grass dried in the sun. Now she looks shyly into his brown eyes. He doesn't look away. He knows she's leaving.

He stamps his foot and crunches a crab apple with big handsome teeth. Then he lets out a trumpeting fart. Laine giggles.

"Quite the charmer, aren't you, Wonder?"

Laine feeds Penelope apples too. When Philip sprung this blue-blooded horse on her, a surprise fourteenth birthday gift, Laine had been offended. It was a declaration that Wonder couldn't compete anymore. With ebony muscles and lusty eyes, Wonder had more soul than any animal in the stable. Thomas always said he'd drink whiskey if you let him at it.

Penelope is a Goody Two-shoes. Her ivory hide unscarred. She holds herself together and apart perfectly. And Laine punished her for months by withholding affection. It was the least act of loyalty she could perform for Wonder. But something in Penelope's eyes begged her. Laine caved.

And it turned out Wonder didn't need Laine to choose. Wonder let Penelope take over. *You* like *chilling and eating sugar cubes, flirting and gossiping,* she accused him. And the horses developed an invisible yoke, both of them amplified and enhanced by the other.

"Okay, you guys," Laine says now, scratching both of their chins.

Then she walks backward, memorizing the stable. Horses had stayed fresh for her when so much else had curdled in the last couple years. No matter what happened, she could ride a horse and he would know, by the honesty of her body, what she was going through and why. She takes a mental photograph: the dank floor, bridles glinting in the sunlight, birds fluttering from rafter to rafter, heads raised above stalls to nod at her.

Chris and Maggie sit on the screened-in porch at "Philip's house," which is how the girls think of it even after living here almost three years. Philip is now in fact in the rose garden out back with two Japanese men in suits. Philip, who speaks nine languages, nods as the taller man gestures in the sun.

A Post-it on the fridge says Thomas called, and he won't be back from Newport to say good-bye but he loves her. *A good example of Thomas Hunt's capacity for contradiction.*

"Laine, did you pack the extra shampoo I left on the bed for you?" her mother trills from the second floor.

"I did," Laine calls back.

Laine rolls her eyes at her sisters as they listen to Polly's Ferragamo flats click above their heads. Since this remarriage, Polly has become like a first lady with folders of menus and meetings with house staff. Laine's bags and boxes are piled by the door. *Let's GET ON WITH IT.* If Laine can run when they get to Wellington, she'll escape that bloat–like a dead mole in a swimming pool–she gets when she skips a day's training. When Polly calls Laine up to the attic, Laine sighs theatrically for her sisters, who giggle.

Polly and Laine stand off in the musty dark. The bulb casts cowardly light on skis, infinite archives, boxes of Christmas ornaments.

"You don't have enough warm coats," Polly insists.

"I just don't think I need more than one, Mom."

"And I think that's ludicrous. There is a *spectrum* of events which you may have to attend, Lainey."

Laine makes a grunt of exasperation, a noise reserved for conversations with her mother. She pushes her hair back, white strands dampening in this hot chamber.

"I just always imagined you taking it with you, Lainey. That's all."

What they're arguing about lies in a snowdrift of Bonwit Teller tissues: It's Polly's camel hair coat from when she was a student at Miss Walker's. On the sideboard downstairs is a photograph of seventeen-year-old Polly with a bob walking a bicycle in Rome, with this coat on. Laine swears she looks content in the portrait, and has always wondered if that was a camera trick or if her mother had at one point been happy.

Laine sees baby blue beneath the beige—another coat. She tosses her mom's over a filing cabinet, and holds up her grandmother's Balenciaga with gold buttons. Elsa was Thomas's mother. A Swede, she passed down this inheritance of blue eyes and white hair to her granddaughters. She was heavy drinking and sinful and stunning, and she laughed like a cougar: all teeth. And there was Polly with shoulder-length brown hair and childish eyes (which are sweet when she's excited and small when threatened), her thinness hard won and tortured: a dud between elegant generations.

"I'll take *this*!" Laine says. "Oh my God, is that Grandpapa's cap?"

She retrieves her grandad's black fisherman's cap, and starts down the ladder in her new finds, until her mom starts coughing. Laine looks up, head level with the wood floor. She stares at her mother's small fist at her mouth.

"Are you okay?" she asks.

"Mnnh," Polly tries, patting her chest, working on a smile, gesturing at the dust. But she doesn't actually answer. "Lainey. I keep meaning to ask you. Did you thank your stepfather? Getting to go away to such a school is really a fine gift."

Should have known that was coming. "I'll do that right now."

Downstairs, the girls are on the porch again, wearing

Speedos and drinking orange juice, hair wet now from swimming and thus a darker blond than Laine's. The sisters used to look so similar they freaked people out. They were variations in B flat, or three sketches someone did of the same girl. Identical sky blue eyes staring without expression from complacent faces. Laine remembers baths together when the three of them, covered in bubbles, were one entity, existing as one soul in warm water.

This summer was pivotal in how each one changed. Maggie babbles in a new way, unthinking and giddy, and compulsively eats sweets, her tummy round in her bathing suit. Christine has "rages," as Philip calls them, a few so severe Polly took her to the doctor. Her bangs are super-short, fixed after Chris cut them with sewing scissors.

"Laine," Maggie says, as usual starting an interaction before she has anything to say, and she tries to think of something. "Are you, um, are you going to bring George with you?"

George the yellow Lab is lying on the flagstone floor, butterscotch chin speckled with white hairs, black rubbery gums wet. "No, George is staying here."

"Where is, um . . . Laine, are you going to take your bed?"

"Nope."

"Then what are you going to sleep on?" Maggie has sneaked over to Laine and now anxiously twirls a strand of her sister's hair.

"They'll give me a bed."

"Who will?"

"The school."

Maggie twists the hair, thinking. "We don't have beds at my school."

"I know." Laine pulls her baby sister onto her lap and smells her neck. She looks over Mag's shoulder and sees an expression on Christine's face. She has never seen anything like it. Although it might have been the same way Laine stared at her father while he packed his bags.

2

Nikki paces her room, Kanye West thumping her eardrums, *XXL* and *GQ* pages torn and taped to the wall. She steps back from the mirror to adjust her thong. Her naked breasts look like they might have bar codes, but no—these monsters are homegrown. "Ba-bye," she says to her reflection.

Then she tries it reggae-dance hall style. "Biddy bye bye."

She bends forward from the waist and blows a kiss like an old-school movie actress, and whispers: "Bye, everybody, thanks for coming out tonight."

Stepping into the gold wedges she bought at a sex store, she cocks her hip, appraises her body: It's tall, voluptuous, the thighs dimpled and legs long. The fake gold anklet shivers as her ankles tremble in the six-inch heels. She turns and cranes her head to see her ass. She practices a sly porn-star-next-door smile. "Bye now. Don't forget me."

Her cell beeps a Lil' Kim tune, and she pulls on sweatpants and a tank as she talks.

"You're a dick; you're late as *usual*, Vanessa!" she shouts and claps the phone shut.

Nikki checks her reflection again, liking the look of herself mad. *Yeah*. Her Bambi eyes are pie sliced with honey yellow, face shaped exactly like a heart. Her luxuriant layers of chestnut hair are recovering from a streaking experiment with Vanessa. Tucked into the mirror's frame: magazine shots of Salma Hayek and Beyoncé, a famous sketch of Ava Gardner, Polaroids of her cat who's dead, a note to diet. Not like she diets. She drinks Diet Cokes, but basically *if I want some IHOP pancakes, that's what I'm going to have. And if I want some Burger King fries, guess what? I think I'll have some Burger King fries.* She storms downstairs, BABY GIRL in calligraphy on her ass. *No one better screw up my big night.*

Nikki traipses through white-carpeted rooms. Victor Olivetti bought this house a day before Nikki was born. He drove his wife and their two-day-old baby, Nicole, here, unloaded his family from the rusted taupe Cadillac into the barren home, gingerly set them in the bedroom, and looked at the new mom with anxiety. She smiled like an exhausted angel.

In the first years, they used cast-off furniture from Victor's uncle's office; they ate spaghetti and meatballs at a glass conference table, seated on folding chairs. For Christmas, her mom got bartered jewelry and Nikki got Chinatown toys. Nikki went with her mom to Goodwill and helped look for clothes without stains. And even now, walking from room to room, Nikki feels the ghost of that younger self trailing along, pulling on her hand like a little sister.

But the North Shore Gravel Company thrived, branched out from tar and rocks to yard statuary, sod, imported Italian swimming pool tile. The house grew these chandeliers, a sauna, marble floors, a laser alarm system. A Maltese named Madonna with a bubble gum pink sphincter and a Louis Vuitton collar. An everyday-but-Sunday maid named Dolores. A white piano in the parlor that no one plays.

Each day at noon Sharon, Nikki's stepmother, serves Victor lunch. He's sitting now in the glass conservatory napping after three courses: Today was braised leeks, pasta carbonara, veal scaloppine. He drinks one tumbler of red wine. To finish he sips espresso with a twist of orange on the saucer. He's not fat and never will be; just a big guy getting bigger. The man owns a gun, chews a toothpick makes the occasional politically incorrect joke, and is cited by everyone who knows him as a sweetheart, a king, the best guy. Nikki looks out a window at the glass room, where Sharon, once his personal trainer, kisses his forehead and removes plates. *What. Ever.*

Many Plainview families came up the way Nikki's did: They moved here from the Bronx, Brooklyn, or Queens, overextended themselves to buy a house or packed three generations into a two-bedroom, and then slowly made money. To parties, kids used to wear polyester suits and powder-blue rayon dresses bought by grandparents still living in Bayside or on Staten Island. There were homemade cupcakes, tape cassettes played on boom boxes, goody bags of wholesale candy. But soon some families saved enough to move on to lavish event halls, ice sculptures, sushi. The Olivettis belong to that subgroup, and tonight's party is catered, gold tables already set up in the yard, buckets of Red Bull chilling behind the bar, a deejay on his way with turntables.

Most, though, still struggle to pay bills. Those Mazdas are leased. Both parents work union jobs. They shop at Sam's Club. They take in stray relatives from the five boroughs. Nikki's house is a castle in comparison, and Sharon's the stray her dad took in, *the stray who became queen. Nice work, Shar.*

If there was a Stepmom Barbie, Sharon would be it. Nikki is certain Sharon got all her new affects from a *Cosmo* article on dealing with a difficult stepdaughter. Like, *does it bother you, do you mind, I don't want to take over, I want you to have your space.* And while Sharon stuttered, Nikki would coldly and obviously analyze the blonde's outfits.

The prewedding week last year was soggy with Nikki's stubbornness. She wouldn't wear the dress Sharon picked, or rehearse. She also, *let's see,* wouldn't smile. *Ever.* Vic had it out with her on the big day, truly thrashing her verbally for the first time in her life. She strew rose petals in the bride's path, quaking like a kicked dog. But that turned quickly to bloodlust for vengeance. Not against her dad, of course.

And this party tonight has lost its identity in that smoke of Nikki's rage. It's become her screw-you-I'll-have-an-expensive-party-too party, but really it's quite something else.

"What's up, girlfriend," Vanessa says when she finally arrives, sticking her chest out in a red tube top, belly ring sparkling, and sucking on a Mocha Frappuccino from Starbucks. "How's my celebrity?"

"I just can't get effing dressed," Nikki deadpans as the girls tromp upstairs. "I have a hundred people about to knock down my door and I'm in sweats. Ness, what the hell?"

"Well, that's where best friends come in. We're going to make you look superhot and sticky."

They're both enjoying acting serious, as though Nikki's due on the red carpet at Cannes. Vanessa's bleached hair is in a high ponytail, eyes lined in black, lips shiny with gloss. Nikki looks Vanessa up and down.

"You look kind of cute," she admits with theatrical and sullen envy. "I need to look cuter."

"Of course you're going to look cuter. It's your show, bitch."

When they hear the electric gate, they run to the window. The pickup has flame-striped Corona boogie boards strapped on top. The girls hold their breath as Tadd and Steve climb out in long basketball shorts, the waistbands of Nautica briefs showing. Steve sets his empty 40 on the grass.

"Don't you know that's *rude*?" Nikki yells scornfully. All heads turn up.

"Yeah, so's flashing your melons out of your family's house," Steve says.

"You wish." Nikki smiles.

He laughs raucously, having done it to piss her off. "Chill, Nik," he says, the scorpion tattoo stark on his forearm in the sun. He drags on his cigarillo and drops it to sizzle in the bottle then sets it on the truck bed.

And then the driver's door slowly opens.

It's Mikey, all six feet and seventeen years of him, Steve's older brother and chauffeur. Shaved head and berry-brown chest, dark nipples. He twirls keys around his finger, then folds his big arms on the roof of the truck and squints up at the girls.

"What it is, ladies?"

Vanessa and Nikki lay back on the carpet, staring at the ceiling.

"He's too hot," they say. "He's just too hot."

Stars shine in a hot blue heaven. Red lanterns sway, globes of light bouncing on wires. The pool shines like a jewel. The deejay, fedora tilted, spins on turntables set up by the diving board. Nikki's parents drink casually in the golden-lit conservatory without looking her way, but they're on point.

Tadd and Steve loiter under pine trees. A red coal on a joint explains the skunky smoke.

"Having fun, Cinderella?" Tadd asks, baseball cap tweaked sideways.

"What the hell does that mean?" Nikki asks, arms folded across her chest, standing close to the boys.

"You know we're going to miss you, Nik." Tadd is the one who really wants to get on tonight.

Steve sends the spliff her way. Nikki rarely smokes, and neither does her girl posse—they leave it to the guys. But she takes a toke. She coughs.

Steve grins behind sunglasses: "Cough and get off."

Everyone's having a decent time but the better time will

be wherever everyone finds themselves next. They'll join some older kids in a yard where the parents aren't home, and the summer will unravel itself just a bit further as couples make out on dew-wet lawns, get too high, throw Doritos at one another, draw a penis on the passed-out kid's forehead. The guys will end up playing a manic game of tag while someone stands off in a corner of the lawn, holding onto a sapling, spitting as he waits to throw up.

Nikki finds herself upstairs, looking down. Some of these kids she's known since the first day she got on the bus, clutching her brown bag of Twinkies and Sunny Delight. Early friends fell by the wayside, though, when Nikki pulled her own Evan Rachel Wood and dropped out of the sleepover circuit to debut on the ecstasy-and-blow-job scene. Not that she kept up with the fastest fast kids. But even tagging along got her in trouble. She and Ness would catch each other's eye at some bad event in a garage or abandoned house: *How many times can we save our own asses before we get unlucky?*

Vanessa and Nikki had watched the magnificent crash and burn of the school's sexiest and craziest girl: Desi Grannelli. At first it was fun and awesome, and then it struck fear into their bowels. Growing up, Desi was the Holy Grail, perfectly sexual at eleven, charmed not just physically but emotionally, romantically, spiritually. At twelve she knew what a man wanted. And then came the group-sex-

and-tequila parties, the speedballs, the abortions. Ness and Nik called her Saint Dead End. *She's dying for our sins.*

Privately Nikki thought of her as a dumb animal that wants to please its cruel master. She glowered at the girl whenever she ran into her at a 7-Eleven or Denny's. *Be better than that.* But the part of Nikki that knew how to keep to a better path, that knew she was never going to be anyone's dog, this part of her was more and more frequently overwhelmed by the part of her that wanted to be a part of everything. Playing with the older guys, who had blossomed last year on Nikki's horizon, meant playing by the guys' rules.

Nikki didn't know the slip-sliding was happening; she only felt off balance, like when you stand up quickly after a long, long sleep. She only felt like *if there's an escape hatch, maybe I should take it.* Besides, leaving was a way to flip off Sharon, as in *you drove me out of the house, bitch, look what you made me do.*

Oh, no, Nikki thinks, getting vertigo now. Looking down she suddenly realizes the magnitude of her decision. She hadn't seen it till now. She misunderstood. She's been throwing it in their faces, her new luxury accessory: Wellington. Boarding school. *Dead Poet's Society* meets *The O.C.* A rich slumber party. A couture academy.

Why do I suddenly feel like the loser here? This is my big night, my bad-ass party. This is the night I was waiting for all summer.

Maybe because this is a good-bye party. Everyone is having a good time *because I'm leaving.*

Nikki wakes to violent red light sliding against her wall, and thinks for a dream-stranded moment that it is night, that the bonfire at the after party is being cast into the room.

But it's sunrise, all shades up. A Poland Spring bottle overturned on the carpet, but she still has cottonmouth. And the TV is blue, the tape she watched when she got home many hours finished. *I can't believe I watched it again,* she thinks with dread. Unable to sleep, Nikki had watched it without sound, ashamed before she even hit play. As always, the images had a sedating, almost narcotizing effect that lasted until she drifted away.

"Hey, Nik," her dad says softly. "Are you up?"

She unlocks the door. He tries to assess her state, as he often does although he's no good at it.

"I'm not going," she tells him, her voice shaky. "This is a mistake."

He sighs as if he'd seen this coming.

Please don't drag us through it again, Dad. Nikki had actually been a Goody Two-shoes. And then came ninth grade. Vic could feel it, last September. His girl was growing up, but he didn't know how, or where, or with whom. It was a sensation, like coming home and immediately knowing an upstairs window was left open and the rain got in.

Dr. Halliday, the shrink they picked just because they heard he was so expensive, suggested Wellington. His daughter Madison had loved it. *Nikki is too bright, Victor, her scores are so high. She's restless because she's smart. She needs fodder, a challenge, a change.* The doctor was an ambassador from another world. They treated him, in his tweeds and cuff links, like an oracle.

"How can it be a mistake if you haven't tried it?" Victor asks now, coming into the room and sitting on her bed as if his weight might break the frame. "You're my big girl. Nik, you're fine."

"I'm so not fine, can't you see?" she says.

Victor composes himself. "If it's just fear, just raw fear, princess, then good. You should be afraid. You don't take risks without feeling the fear. You think my parents didn't feel it when they came over here? What, you think this place welcomed them? You think it was comfortable for me to start North Shore Gravel from scratch, from nothing? You don't think signing papers is scary, Nik? Signing away your life?"

His voice gets more Brooklyn as he gets upset. He gestures with enormous hands.

"Nik, do this for me. Make it to Christmas. Give it a shot, princess."

She looks at her dad with doe eyes, grabs hold of one of his hands with both of hers like she did when she was little. It goes both ways in this family, the concessions: Nikki will do anything she can for her father, even though she knows she can't give him what he wants either. *Stop. Don't be like this. Just hush.*

"Okay," she says.

He looks her over, trying to gauge the nature of her surrender. But she's mysterious to him. He'll simply accept.

"God, this is scary," she says, looking at the room she's lived in her whole life. Where she clomped around in a Little Mermaid nightgown and her mom's Gucci stilettos. Where she wet the bed. Cried. Dreamed. Where she sat around with girlfriends and ate Pop Tarts, did homework, scratched names and hearts into the molding, performed séances, learned tricks from porn stolen from someone's older brother, whitened teeth while combing dolls' hair. Her room now seems small and tawdry and also as big as the galaxy, holding life and death between its walls. "For real."

"It's me and Sharon who are sad, Nik, we got it the hardest. *You're* leaving *us*."

She looks up and her face is wet. *Hush, please, just stop talking.*

"You'll leave but then you'll come back, and I swear to you we'll always be here waiting, sweetie."

Nik smiles through tears, but they both know he just said the wrong thing. No one can make that promise.

3

Who knew a trip to destiny would begin on the Long Island Expressway? The Escalade's grille is gold like gangster teeth. Nikki lies in the backseat, feet pressing against the window, and sings along with Green Day. The traffic is horrible near the bridge, the city distant like Oz. Cinders drift.

Nikki looks at Sharon's head: *You get him to yourself now, are you happy?*

Once they hit the interstate, Nikki begs for ice cream. She doesn't even want it, but she's using up the coupons of childhood in fear they won't be good next time she's home.

Vic meets her eyes in the rearview. "Baby. It's eight in the morning."

"So-o-o-o-o?"

"I have to break it down for you, what to eat when? You never learned, in all the years we been eating breakfast in the morning and dessert at night?"

"Daddy, it's my *last meal*; I should get whatever I want."

"Now you're on death row?"

"Then an Egg McMuffin," Nikki negotiates without pause.

In the graffitied McDonald's bathroom, Nikki writes her own name with eye pencil on the mirror. Sapphire letters over her reflection. *How old am I, ten? What a retarded thing to do.* But it feels good to leave a record, like Gretel dropping bread crumbs. When she comes out, Sharon is leaning against the building, puffing on a skinny menthol, holding something.

Sharon exhales smoke, shifts in her white jeans. Nikki stares at her stepmom with dead eyes, waiting. *I'm going to get some life advice from Miss December here, who's never been farther than effing Atlantic City.*

"Nik?" Sharon asks, grinding out the cigarette with her shoe.

Nikki deadens her eyes even more—past dead, to the afterlife. She's had, let's just say, a bit of practice at this. "What."

"I gotta tell you. If you don't want to do this, you just say the word. Your dad is acting like a tough guy, but you could knock him off this plan with a feather today. That's between you and me."

Nikki is too surprised to keep her poker face. For a minute, she looks like the girl Sharon first met four years ago.

"Well, thanks for the info. We're kind of halfway there, though . . ." Nikki doesn't know what to say—a historical event—and lets her sentence fade. She looks at the Escalade, shining in greasy orange sunlight, the highway smogging the world beyond. "What's in the bag?"

Sharon holds it up and makes a lopsided smile. "Ice-cream."

They follow winding roads where leaves droop off trees in the heat. In gritty yards are battered lake boats on trailers, fluorescent kids' toys. Unlit Christmas lights hang from gutters. Two obese redheads who look like sisters drink from soda cans and watch the SUV go by, their babies playing in ochre grass at their big feet. Spooky ginger sunbeams rip through trees and spotlight the dry earth.

"Ew, this is Deliverence-ville," Nikki scoffs, but quietly, in deference.

"The journey is half the experience, princess."

"Tell me this isn't the town."

"This isn't the town. We got about thirty, thirty-five miles to go."

They pass through Litchfield, Connecticut, its homes

crisp and ornate as if cut from white paper. On a houseless stretch of road, a deer's head is twisted back on its neck, purple intestines baking on asphalt.

In Glendon, Connecticut, home to Wellington, they go by the apothecary shop, a church glistening like an iced cake, a red firehouse, the old-fashioned gas station where a teen with a buzz cut waits in the shade of a maple for cars to pump. A Chinese restaurant built like a pagoda. Daisies blooming. Everything shiny like a toy set taken out of a box and buffed with a cloth.

Nikki's lips get dry as a golf course snakes along the road. Elms tower. Fields glisten with health. The dormitories rise on the hill. The Escalade is driving up the page of a brochure, and it turns through an iron gate burned with the Wellington crest, cruises up Monroe Drive.

They park on the lawn next to a car with Kansas plates, its back door opened like a musty mouth breathing out the long, sunbaked ride. As Sharon steps out of the Escalade, the rhinestones spelling *Spoiled* on her T-shirt shimmer. Nik reaches for Vic's hand and they all walk, in shock.

Holy prestige with an effing capital P.

The eight dorms have stood on either side of Monroe Drive for two centuries, and they have surrendered to their face-off. These buildings stare at a space just above the other's head, like opposing pieces on a chessboard. On the boys' side, Cadwallader lies in the shadow of Eliot, whispering in its ear. Summer is covered in ivy and stands apart, in the sun. Blackstick is enormous, robust, jovial—its many windows spying on the whole campus.

On the other side are girls' dorms. Laundry-room steam billows out of the basement window of Gray, and Thornfield stands with good posture behind it. Appleby is the shyest of the four, ringed by rhododendron bushes, the front door opening and closing. And there's Lancaster, with its bald, wide face. It's mammoth, and Nikki approaches it like a building in a dream that's unfamiliar but you're supposed to know it.

"Welcome home, cupcake," Vic says.

"Yo, this looks like Papi's mausoleum at the cemetery."

Nikki slows as they near the fourth floor, letting her bag drag. Girls and parents chatter by with trunks, but Nikki suddenly can't hear anything more than her heart. The lip-gloss pot falls out of her pocket, and she asks a tall, tawny-haired girl to pick it up.

"Would you grab that?" Nikki tells her.

The girl hesitates before kneeling and gives her a look, but Nikki doesn't notice it and just takes the gloss.

Because someone is in Nikki's room—407—a shadow on the wall. Nikki got the name of her roommate in July, and examined the letter as though it was her betrothal. Sharon and Vic hover at the threshold. Nikki blunders in, blood roiling, humiliated that everyone has to be involved in this bizarrely intimate moment.

Sometimes destiny is a person, not a place.

"Hi, I'm Laine."

"Hey, what's up! I'm Nikki."

The girls immediately throw invisible tape measures around each other, as if they were tailors. Laine's unable to disguise her feelings, like a polite child disappointed in a Christmas present. Nikki panics, unwilling to deal with Laine's big blue eyes.

"Shit, this is tiny. Don't you think?"

Laine shrugs. "I guess. Do you have a preference of bed?"

"Nah," Nikki says, throwing her fake Fendi bag on a mattress, hurtling into action to distract everyone from tension. "They both suck. Gross. This is *Girl, Interrupted* or some shit, right?"

Laine tries a smile.

"I can't believe this place costs thirty grand. I mean, where's my terry cloth bathrobe, right? Show me a little free shampoo."

Laine looks at this creature in glittery eye shadow, lying on raw bed with hair in a fan as if she'd woken up in a stranger's room after a night of partying. *I might have pulled the short straw.*

Vic offers to take them to lunch. Nikki tells him he *has* to head, but looks at him with the puppy eyes she made on the first day of kindergarten. Laine tries not to watch the family's gooey good-byes; it's one step short of heavy petting. Especially when Dad hands over the black AmEx.

"Emergencies," he stresses, holding tight to the card as his daughter giggles, and he waits for her to act serious before he lets go.

Laine's family could buy the Olivettis a thousand times over, and Polly left her with a ten-dollar bill and a shoulder pat. When Polly vanished from the room—and vanished is how it felt, complete, sudden, magical, even though it was not sudden—Laine had what is a rare moment for her. Watching Polly's midnight-blue linen shoulders turn away and slip through the door, Laine knew she would remember the moment forever. That's where her thought began and ended. She would have denied feeling terrified or sad, *because I'm neither. I just know I'll remember that visual for a long time. What?*

"All righty, all righty then," Vic says, until Sharon takes his hand and they leave.

"So, I'm going to head over to the barbecue. See you there?" Laine is making her first break.

"I'll go with you!"

Great.

They leave the room on a blind date. Outside, canvas totes and Pierre Deux duffels are still tumbling out of

Volvos, BMWs, Range Rovers. And trailing students is a wake of good-byes, lectures, cheeks pinched by worried mothers, spices and crumbs from favorite meals served last night in dining rooms all over the world.

"So how'd you find out about this place?" Nikki asks as they walk.

"Well, I've known a lot of people who went here."

"Are you serious? You're the first boarding school kid I ever met."

They're starting to finally evaluate each other. *WOW.* Laine stares: Nikki's legs are *shrink-wrapped* in bright blue denim, cheeks dusted pastel pink, eyes war painted. A South Beach hoodie ending at midriff. Gum. Stripper heels. And parents who may pay tuition in unmarked bills. *Looks like I'm shacking up with Meadow Soprano.*

Nikki sees a cross between a Tommy Hilfiger girl—with the rugby shirt and Nantucket bracelet, the deep tan and pert nose—and a young German boy. *Put some lederhosen on this little fella and she'll be the toast of every pedophile chat room on the web.*

The girls walk past two scholarship guys, one Puerto Rican and the other Indian, sitting on the Blackstick steps. They came up early on a Greyhound, moved in their few bags, and didn't know what to do after. They're trying to look relaxed, following a Frisbee game, but their eyes are guarded, defensive. Nikki is about to make eye contact with them, and they with her, and at the last minute both parties slide their eyes away. The outsiders don't sense each other.

"Seen any hot guys yet?" Nikki asks Laine, having almost crashed into a sapling as she gets her bearings.

"I haven't really been looking."

There's innocent contraband being smuggled into dormitories: teddy bears and stuffed tigers and baby blankets. The sweater from Grammy, worn constantly at home, carefully folded, that will be put on once here and never again after the taunts. And the not so innocent: a pack of Reds, condoms pilfered from an older brother, a half gallon of supermarket vodka. The kids boarding since sixth grade at Indian Mountain or Eaglebrook or somewhere in Switzerland know to stow rum in a shampoo bottle, weed in a carved-out dictionary, the log of Copenhagen in a golf bag. They're professionals.

"So, like, do you have brothers and sisters?" Nikki asks, heels sinking into the hill.

"Two sisters," Laine says.

"I'm an only child," Nikki offers without being asked. "Where you from?"

"Greenwich."

"Is that like near London?"

Laine just looks at her. *This would be funny except it's not. Keep saying things like that and you'll be sitting by yourself, no way anyone here is going to let you get away with being so retarded.*

35

The sun ripples red across the lake, which is expansive and deep, affecting the land for miles with its stillness. Teachers drink lemonade, talk with students. On the raft older kids dive, flirt, splash and pose. Grill smoke gusts in the wind across the gingham-clothed table laden with fried chicken, sandwiches, chips, burgers, hot dogs, salad, sodas. Usually Laine handles a social scene by being invisible. *Just answer questions, smile, be polite.* Escape the jaws of small-talk death. *But with this guido Lindsay Lohan for a wingman, those days are over.* She enters the picnic with head down, as though she'd invited Nikki here and only now realized her error.

All the new students mill about in the gentle, woodsy afternoon. And this is how things begin: like a pack of cards thrown with force and almost sadistic fun into the air, and they fall where they fall, the jokers and aces, the low cards and high cards, the hearts, the diamonds, the jacks.

Nikki looks around as they stand on line. *Everyone* is in Umbros or khakis and Izods. At least Nikki feels guys check her out; *boys will be boys, thank effing heavens.* Nikki adjusts her bra and Laine stares.

"Oh, eat me." Nikki laughs. "I mean, they're *heavy*, you know what I'm saying? Sometimes I got to reconfigure." *Is she going to stare at me like this all semester?*

The two girls load up their plates and float to a picnic table, making shy hellos to the four boys sitting there. Without even knowing they're doing it, the two girls jockey for power: Nikki by being too loud and Laine by being silent.

A tall kid with black curly hair and creamy skin, wearing faded surf shorts and a My Morning Jacket shirt, dumps cole slaw from his plate onto Nikki's.

"Gee, thanks, I didn't even want any." Nikki grins.

"I made it myself." Noah pouts.

Laine silently cuts the skin off chicken leg, but the guy next to her speaks up, his beard scruffy, hair cornrowed. Greg's tank reveals tattoos—the ink is Braille on his black skin.

"You ain't eating too much," he says.

"Uh, yeah. Not so hungry, I guess. Do you work here?"

Greg smirks. "Nah, just a new student like you, ma. I'm Greg. Nice to meet you."

Laine's face flushes. "I'm Laine. I just didn't know because, well, you look older."

He nods, already looking away: "You all right, don't sweat. I'ma grab another soda. Anyone want something?"

Laine sits across from a guy gripping a Sidekick II—which are illegal, but no one pays him mind. His plate is untouched, an empty coffee cup beside it.

Minutes pass until Laine introduces herself.

"My name is Gabriel. Hello." He speaks softly and with a heavy accent. He turns to his game. His blue Armani shirt dark along the collar with heat, chocolate mole above his lip on olive skin.

Noah is ridiculing Nikki's Long Island accent. She loves the attention. Noah thumps the fourth guy, Chase, on the back when he makes a joke.

Chase coughs and finally joins the conversation. "Bro, easy. I'm chewing here, let a man eat," he drawls.

With honey-streaked long hair and shirttails out, Chase slouches elegantly. Nikki watches as he waves back to upperclassmen jumping off the raft. Nikki can't make out their calls. New students and old arrive at the same time to Wellington, but the new kids are doomed to these orientation events while returning students circle like tigers. Nikki spots a dark-haired guy lowering himself into the water. Veins in his biceps pop as he holds himself up—Nikki can tell he's older. He grins into the sun, face pale and strong, and Nikki has trouble looking away. He's with a bunch of guys, all of them built and shirtless. *This is a freaking Abercrombie & Fitch ad.*

Nikki grabs the label of Chase's button-down shirt for lack of something better to do. "What the fuck is Ben Silver? The store where your daddy shops?"

"It's in Charleston, sweetie, Charleston. Where you from, Nikki?"

"Long Island."

Noah says she seems to be a long way from home.

"What do you mean?" Nikki protests. "Chase is from

South Carolina."

Chase asks Nikki who her roommate is, and Nikki points, mouth full of cheeseburger: "Right there," she mumbles. "That's Laine."

Chase says: "Laine Hunt? Ah, you're like a field hockey star, right? My friend Casey was at training camp with you. I'm Chase. Pleasure."

And this is when the scales groan irretrievably to Laine's side of the table.

Noah extends his hand. "Hey, how's it going? Noah. I think I know your cousin Randall."

"Nice to meet you," Laine says.

A senior named Heather rushes up the path from the lake to hug Laine. Her red hair dark from being wet, round face dotted with orange freckles as if by a kid with a crayon. Her armpits bunched up with bluish flesh at the crease, bikini strap digging. Nikki notices a black toenail, too. *Pippi Longstocking got beat with the ugly stick.*

"I thought I heard your voice! Where ya been, stranger? Are you so ready for practice tomorrow? You know she's going to make us puke, right?"

Then Heather says hi to Chase, asks Noah how his sister is. Nikki stares at her, wondering where on earth she came from.

"Is that your crew out there on the raft? Those dudes are totally hot," Nikki says, blundering into the conversation.

Heather takes a moment to appraise. "My 'crew'?" She laughs. "Yeah, *sistah*, that's my crew. Peace out yo."

Everyone laughs, and Heather turns to the raft to communicate something with her stance. The tawny-haired girl that Nikki asked to pick up her lip gloss is squinting. Heather turns back, smiling smugly, and continues comparing summer notes with the others.

"How do you guys know each other?" Nikki asks the group, trying again, a band of Dior sunglasses clenched in her teeth, but no one answers. *What had I thought, that they all would be strangers to each other?* Yes, she had. She had imagined a person from every state, wearing banners like pageant contestants. Introducing themselves and trading stories about cool lives back home.

A band of amethyst burns through black trees. Dr. Halliday once told her to keep a diary to help slow down. *I'm not a freakin' human typewriter.* So he said that once a day, she should at least stop and get her bearings. *I don't want to look at a clock like a freaking soldier and figure my shit out at fourteen hundred hours or something.* Okay, then. Pick something natural, like sunset. When the sun sets, ask yourself how you feel.

So how do you feel right now, Nicole Olivetti?

"Yo, *yo*." Greg suddenly and violently shrugs; but what had frightened him was just a moth—the pale green wings grazed his tattoos. He realizes his overreaction and seems mortified for a second, then laughs. A couple guys join, and by doing so weave gauze over the incident.

Nikki feels more alone now than when she arrived.

Walking back up the hill to the dorms, the new kids are suddenly shy. The headmaster's house looms in the quiet, a sconce bright by the door. The lake glitters from a back window through a front one. A tree's shadow trembles against clapboard. When she looks back, Laine sees a boat turned into the wind to dock, sails painted bloody purple by sunset. The returning students are much more relaxed, from summers spent lifeguarding or hiking mountains with Outward Bound or selling ice cream on Martha's Vineyard, and from not having to do the work of introducing themselves to one another now. Their silhouettes linger by the water's edge, laughter twinkling up through woods, as they let the new students leave first.

Some kids grab tall grasses out of nervous energy as they walk. Bats slice through twilight. Everyone resolutely walks as though they've walked this way before.

They did get a campus map with their welcome package, and most studied it, looking for secret signs to their future:

You are here, walking up a path at dusk with people you don't know yet.

Up that dotted line, in Building X, you will learn something that will change your life.

Where that red dot is you will be kissed.

There, in that blank space near Location 3, you will break someone's heart.

At Location 7 you will get sick after a hard practice. At 9 you will get sick from huffing.

You will be humiliated on the third floor of Building Y.

And there, in that black clearing, you will find yourself.

Now the glass doors of the main building reflect the dusky faces. The group catch themselves in that mirror before the doors are opened, and Nikki and Laine are both shocked to be part of an exotically new whole.

The girls unpack, the night windows starless, quiet. As they empty their boxes, the room is transformed by belongings, and the boxes devolve from packages, containers of life, transitions—into refuse, cardboard broken down and stacked in the stairwell landings.

407. It will be the footnote number to Laine and Nikki's year.

This door will estimate their days and nights here, their relationship quantified by its

being opened and closed, or slammed, or left wide-open.

Rooms don't have locks at Wellington. And so there are no keys.

4

Orientation is really to wear out students and minimize homesickness. Make them too tired to be sad. It's a hellish three days for everyone except the most extroverted freaks who eat this stuff for breakfast. It's a cliché-fest of trust-fall exercises and date-rape seminars and games to learn names. *My name is Nikki, I like Urban Decay makeup, guys with hot trucks, and underage drinking, and I'm from Long Island!*

Many people already know Laine, though. Or know which members of her extended family own which islands or *Fortune* 500 companies. At orientation breakfast a girl mentions the Colony Club portrait of Elsa.

"You look *exactly* like her, I mean, it's frightening."

"Yeah, I've been told that," Laine says.

Her father revered his mother, and so did Fairfield County and Manhattan. Elsa wore sapphire earrings and a white mink with her name stitched in italics inside, and always had chocolates in her handbag for Laine. She called her granddaughter Country Laine and Lovers Laine, since English was still a game to her, and played with Laine for hours.

Once, at the Palm Beach house, Laine found a silver shoe under the couch. Polly took it, shaking her head, turning pink: *They were fox-trotting till six this morning, the whole lot of them. That woman . . .*

Polly is perhaps the only un-famous relative in the family. Prim, solid Polly.

Elsa used to roll her eyes at Polly who scoured the kitchen floor on all fours as if in penance. The mystery of the divorce, since it was still an unsolved crime to Laine, hinged on their discord. Which wasn't possible; Polly served Thomas with papers, not Elsa. But Laine, in figuring out what happened to her family, plays back scenes like the fox-trot incident all the time, digging for secrets. She often thinks of Elsa's funeral. She'd demanded to be buried in a couture ballgown, the folds of which—whispery and as rusty orange as peanut skins—barely fit in the casket. And how Polly cried harder than anyone there, cried in an ugly way, bucking, hiccupping, like a hysterical child.

Laine finds herself thinking about this now, at breakfast.

Interesting. Guess I didn't leave the divorce behind.

Because the thing about going away and leaving things behind is that then their *absence* becomes a presence. Filing into their orientation groups, name tags pinned to shirts, everyone starts to process what it means to be apart from family. No one calls upstairs to you when the phone rings, or when your waffles pop out of the toaster. Dinner doesn't waft into your room, and if it did it wouldn't be pesto the way your dad makes it, or the chicken parm you got once a week that's to die for. There's no morning noise of flushing and shaving that's evolved over the years into a rhythm or melody you know.

Now they all know what family *was*. It was feeling the vibration of the garage door as the early parent left and you still dozed in bed. It was the taste of milk from the carton. It was knowing that the toys you would never ever play with again were in a box in the dark basement, a box with your name on it. Your box.

The few days of orientation are a thrust of new information on every front. Everyone gets Facebooks—portfolios of students' photographs grouped by year, hometown addresses cited below. They identify one another, starting with those who stand out: the white guy wearing a UK-flag tie (*Jeremy Landon, Bermuda, Lower-form*), the stocky Colombian kid whose last name everyone knows from the news lately

(*Gabriel Velez, Lower-form*), the girl with the orange streak painted into her black hair (*Regan Benton, Austin, Texas, Prep*) or the kid with cornrows *(Greg Jenson, Brooklyn, New York, Lower-form)*.

New students, or "newbies," get schooled on why they're lucky to be at Wellington in a welcome speech in the auditorium. Dean Talliworth, in tweedy academic glory, takes the podium. The mike hums as he scans the crowd.

"Future American presidents have sat in your seats. Senators. Olympic champions. Men and women who have changed the world—literally. Being here is a privilege—but it's one you have to live up to every day. Skip a day of striving and you're running behind, you're playing catch up. We chose you, as we chose each student who went on to become an illustrious alum, because we believe you have the *potential* for Wellington character."

The congregation stares. He's a new father to please, for some, and for others a new father to defy. Many students already see this man, just by his stance and pulpit baritone, as a reverend of discipline. Some glow with the attention he's paying to them, and some glow with derision, almost blushing to be lumped or corralled into his new family. Nikki, from her vantage point, can't identify this guy. He's an unknown quantity, and part of her wants to buy into this prestigious endeavor he's advertising, but it feels weird to be invited and bullied simultaneously. Laine, on the other hand, knows dozens of Talliworths. *He means what he says, for better or worse.*

And throughout these meetings and speeches, at lunch tables or in the snack bar, everyone learns the talk. A Prep is a freshman, a Lower-form is a sophomore, an Upper-form is a junior, and Seniors are Seniors. The class doubles in size Lower-form year, so there are as many new kids in that class as there are entering the school as Preps. PGs are Post-graduates, supremely athletic kids who graduated elsewhere and come to Wellington for a cherry to top their college application in exchange for helping a team. Add *in locos parentis* and *No Second Chance Drug and Alcohol Rule* to the lexicon, along with *Gentleman's C* (the assertion that an A anywhere else equals a C here) and *slashes* (demerits for dress code violations or tardiness) and *feeds* (when a dorm-head gives kids food in the hall) and *foos* (when a guy is ambushed by other guys, stripped of all clothes in a minute, then left in the grass, alone), and tack on *fatigue, stress, crush, love, confusion, friendship,* and *loneliness* while you're at it.

By the last day of orientation, Nikki can't take anymore ups and downs. But then she buys books at the campus store. The chemical smell when she opens the pages reminds her of sitting on the linoleum kitchen floor, while her mom smoked and talked on the phone and occasionally stopped stirring sauce to rub Nikki's head absentmindedly, and meticulously taping Spice Girls textbook wrappers onto her new books. It was *a September happiness*. She hasn't felt like this in a few years.

She heads to the dining hall, the first time she's gone by herself, and stands on the periphery. *Jesus,* Nikki thinks, not sure what she's afraid of.

It's not like she didn't deal with cliques back home. In fact, the 2,600-student high school was complex, with basic groups (Losers, Popular Kids, Bullies, Victims)—and factions within each group. Victorian Goths, different from Edwardian Goths. Football players who did charity work. Kif-heads who took the train to museums in the city every weekend. The Alloy Rims and Alizé gangbangers. White girls with cornrows. Dorky gamers who were walking directories of online porn.

But Nikki can't fathom this new system. The racial breakdown is hard-core but unfamiliar. There are lots of non-white kids, but she makes a joke to one black kid, and he answers in a proper British accent with no idea what she's talking about. A couple girls she thinks are Mexican are actually Saudi Arabian royalty. The Jamaican PG soccer players sit in the main room with the most powerful kids. The one table in the corner with no white kids is all scholarship from the Bronx, Brooklyn, Detroit, Chicago and Harlem—they're more isolated than any clique back home. There's an invisible razor-wire fence around that table.

Two distinct tables radiate power from the middle of the room, lit by the skylight. These are the kings and queens. One set is more athletic and straight-laced: the future I-bankers of America. A tawny-haired girl holds court at this table. The other group is deviant, slouchy, more arty and druggy, but when their education and families are through with them, they'll be I-bankers too. The guy from the raft is sprawling on a chair pushed out from the table. These groups don't butt heads. They share power, unwilling to take a chance by starting something. There are floaters, too, people who hop from one circle to the other, who eat their meatloaf at one table and cupcake at the other.

Nikki is overwhelmed by these two tables. Because they own the world right now; they're at the peak, they're stars. Eyes bright with fire, bodies full of sex, skin pure and gleaming. They flirt, joke, and electrify the place. They make any teacher, even the youngest, look withered, disappointed, enslaved as they are by tenure track and car payments and reality. They are Seniors. They exist thousands of feet above Nikki, unable to see her when they look down. They are wild and free and beautiful.

That evening, Nikki sees the housemaster in the hall, and his springer spaniel snarls, hair on its back raised in a ridge.

"By gosh, Nicole," Mr. Lensk says, disturbed. "I should have asked if you're okay with dogs. Are you afraid?

Sometimes that's what it is, they sense fear, you know . . ."

"No, I'm not afraid," Nikki says. Because she never had been before.

When he opens his apartment door, Nikki catches a whiff of saffron, and sees a red Chinese trunk. The home is golden, shining, and the door closes.

In the dorm room, Laine says hello at the same time Nikki asks how her day is. They laugh, try again.

"How was *your* day—"

"How's it going—"

They speak simultaneously again. Nikki would continue but Laine waves it off. "Oh, never mind, right?"

Nikki assumes her roommate has been so *un-roommately* because orientation is stressful, and things will change when school properly starts tomorrow. But the cookies and *Good Luck* note Nikki left yesterday still sit on Laine's desk, untouched.

Nikki settles into bed in her Victoria's Secret nightgown, starts filing her nails. Laine marks a date book at her desk. Nikki stopped asking questions after getting delayed and short replies, and is shocked at how this hurts. She's watched Laine enough, and doesn't understand why Laine won't give her the time of day. Every time Nikki brings up a guy, or puts on lipstick in the mirror, pungent rejection wafts up from her roommate, even if Laine isn't looking or listening. *It's effing automatic.* After years of playing dress-up princess, Nikki's finally encountering the real thing. The blond blue-eyed girl who needs no boyfriend, has no fears, and bears no scars.

Nikki has a fat scar up her shin from a meaningless rusty jungle gym accident when she was four. The stitches left a zipper mark, as though one could undo this wound and extract the incident, haul up the pain from that long ago day. And that's just one mark. There's the cigarette burn from that Sublime cover band night at the Beacon. The slice on her stomach from the water slide. *I could go on.*

Someone raps on the door before check-in that night.

"Hey, girls," the tawny-haired girl says, a green apple Blow Pop in her cheek, when Laine opens the door.

Oh shit, here she is. Laine has been expecting her. Schuyler Covington is notorious, bicoastal, sociopathically pretty. Her dad produced a portion of his generation's biggest films, and she's A-listed at Element and Hyde, seated immediately at any restaurant. And on the East Coast, she belongs to tennis and beach and yacht and country and squash and dining clubs since her mom's a Rockefeller once removed. Now she wears boxers and a ripped lacrosse shirt from a past boyfriend, diamond studs in her ears. Her skin is summer-teak, pin-straight hair tawny, and legs bony. Laine saw her in Newport this summer—Schuyler barefoot in a sundress, on a porch misty with smoke from her cigar, moon rustling in grasses, with older men drinking and laughing.

"I can't *believe* I'm your proctor!!"

"Yeah, this will be so fun," Laine says. "Schuyler, this is Nikki."

"Nikki, what's up?"

Nikki smiles, sits up higher in bed. "Not much. How do you guys know each other?"

Schuyler says: "You know, Nantucket, field hockey camp, all that stuff. Where you from, Nikki?"

"Long Island."

"Hamptons?" Schuyler asks.

"No, Plainview, Nassau County."

Schuyler actually laughs. "How *nice*. Yeah, you told me to pick up your lip gloss when you moved in, maybe you don't remember. And you know I think my friend Heather met you at the picnic; you made, like, an *incredible* impression!"

"Where are you from?" Nikki says.

Schuyler is now pulling Laine out of the room. "I'm just going to borrow your roommate! Carry on with your manicure. Great to meet you!"

When they're out in the hall, Schuyler shakes Laine's shoulders. "Ohmygod, you got shafted." She looks laughingly into Laine's eyes, pretending to try to get herself to be serious. "You got *so* shafted. I'm so sorry."

Laine nervously looks at the door, worried Nikki can

hear. "I know," she mutters.

Now as they walk the hall, Schuyler points at her own flip-flops, even though Laine wasn't looking at them and didn't mention them. "Calypso. So *cute*, right?"

"Yeah."

"I'm gonna give you the VIP tour, my friend."

401. "That's Heather; she's a bitch and she's my best friend and coproctor. We both have fridges so give me food you need to stash. No one else is allowed."

402. "And this is Aya; she's *Japanese*." She says this in an overly polite, I'm-just-not-going-to-go-into-it voice. "She likes, how to say it, *the art life,* and kind of believes that maybe that's all that exists in the world." A girl with a bob hangs a violet lantern, books spread on her floor.

403. "That's Jen and Nina." Schuyler mouths: "*Lovers. Since they were Preps.* It seems weird, but everyone here ends up giving it a try."

Laine looks at Schuyler with alarm.

Schuyler sucks her lollipop and laughs. "I'm messing with you, Lainer! I mean, you *know* there's girl-on-girl action happening behind closed doors *somewhere*, but who knows where?"

404's door glows with green light. "Lower-form, been locked in there all day. Got special permission for a lizard. Dawn something or other, biggest freak on the block."

They pass a jock girl in 405 pulling grass from a pair of

cleats and a thin, sickly girl. "Polar opposites. Kat is dumb as a rock and Madeline wears black and recites French poems about dead people, but they're, like, best buddies."

406. Charlotte and Parker are unpacking. "New girls."

407 is Nikki and Laine. Schuyler says loudly: "That's you and your little badda-bing friend."

In 408 two blond girls straighten their hair with an iron and eat popcorn. "Southern girls. You'd think they were all innocent and shit but these girls are hand-job queens, I'm talking zero to sixty in thirty seconds. The boys call them 'happy ending gals.' But play nice. Doctors down south still hand out pills like candy so these girls can get you better grades, make you skinny, and keep you stoned."

Schulyer's room has plants, a faux snakeskin beanbag chair, a signed poster of *Apocalypse Now.* "Francis gave it to me for my birthday, isn't that *rad?*"

On the corkboard, a *Town & Country* picture of Schuyler in a silver dress with Lauren Bush. "This is mi casa, Lainer! Sucks, compared to what we're used to, right, babe? But you do what you can."

Yeah, you do what you can. As they're leaving the room, Laine sees an album. "What's that?" she asks, and will always wish she'd never wondered.

Schuyler's eyes open and meet Laine's. "I know you're cool, Lainer. But you *cannot* tell anyone about this. Okay?"

Schuyler pats her bed and they both sit down. Laine

doesn't know what to expect. This girl doesn't entice people to look at her or to love her—she *makes* them. She knows how, too, having grown up in flux—between coasts, between worlds, coming of age among masters of personality. Laine is no match. The scary part of Schuyler is that once she's captured a person, she doesn't always know what to do. Like a general taking towns, but unable to remember why—should I liberate the townfolk, or burn them down?

The cover is cracking, pages brown. On the front, words are carved: THE CRASH TEST. Laine looks to Schuyler. *I have a feeling she's going to burn someone down. I hope it's not me.*

"This has been a tradition since the first female class graduated in 1978. Every year it's passed to five girls—five seniors—who make bets on which new girl will leave first."

"Are you serious?"

"Check it out. This book is a work of art. It's a chronicle of what it takes to make it here." The pages are collages of handwriting, documents, school newspaper cutouts. "These are classic. Like in 1982, this is Lecici. Ghetto scholarship kid who came back from Thanksgiving with lice and infected the whole dorm. Trust me, I am so not racist, but look at her!"

Laine looks at a photograph torn from a Facebook: a girl with a stiff, sideways ponytail and a crooked grin, pointed collars on a white uniform shirt. "Wow. You know, maybe I shouldn't see this yet, before I'm—"

"Don't be silly. And don't feel like you're getting *pulled into it;* you're not."

"I know, I know, it's just—"

"And do you want to know the only rule? Not one of us can interfere with the girls' downward spirals; they have to fail on their own. We just watch. Do you know how innocent that is compared to what *guys* do to each other? Besides, my father contributed like half a mil to Boys & Girls of L.A. this year, you know what I mean? It's not like I'm racist. But Lecici was packing her bags pretty quickly. Do you know what I mean?"

Imagine being rich enough to be racist and *conscientious.* "So these are all girls who left early?"

"Yeah, or were bet on as girls who *might* leave early. There's Shannon, 1989, who took like *one too many* hits of acid and wrote 'I'm a good girl' all over her wall. I like this one, too. 1996. Juana from Texas. Took this other girl's monogrammed robe and stood there, after being accused of stealing it, and swore it was her own. With another girl's initials on it. *Love it.*"

"Who's that?"

"Annie Banks. They called her Annie Bangs. She was just annoying."

"Really?"

Schuyler's eyes cloud. "Yeah. Although it's weird—I knew her before we got here, like friends almost, and I

couldn't understand what was so offensive. But then I totally got it after a while, I guess."

There's an awkward silence, so Laine asks: "Who did
you guys bet on this year?"

"Well, not all the bets are in, but I know a couple girls
picked Dawn Fenway, the lizard girl. Then there's Caroline
Camper, who totally thinks she's Janis Joplin, but meanwhile
she's not a rock star, she's just fat and ugly, you know what
I'm saying, Lainer? Ummmm, that Aussie girl Anette, who's
got bipolar written all over her, she'll probably get one bet.

"Of course," Schuyler continues, "I think *my* girl is
going to win."

Nikki's Facebook picture stares out at Laine: smile glossy,
eyes lined in the war paint she puts on to be beautiful.

Sleeping in a room with a stranger is hard. Sleeping in a
room with someone you know has been marked is harder.
As much as Laine feels sorry for her, she wishes she lived
with someone who didn't cause trouble.

Tonight Laine and Nikki hear each other breathe in the
dark. In fact, the whole building breathes, hisses, turns. The
moon casts lavender light on the floor. Even though they're
both exhausted, the girls tip into troubled, shallow sleep.

Nikki had discovered carvings in her wood closet dating
back a hundred years: *Henry loves Sadie. Brad Buzz was here
12/2/51. Drain the Well. Lucas is hot as hell!!!* As dreams suck

her down, her dream self cuts *Nikki* into her own wooden forehead.

For Laine, phantoms in pajamas crowd the room. Schoolboys in nightcaps with candlesticks lean over her bed, the mattress saturated with nightmares and wet dreams, homesickness and exhaustion, love. The ghosts of kids who slept on this iron-framed bed away from home.

Meanwhile, outside, a fox zigzags her red way across the grounds, caring nothing for borders, for the human beings in the dark beds in the identical rooms in the old buildings. Just running by her sense of things—the smell of earth, the glitter of moonlight, hunger, the prospect of killing something, organic curiosity. Not carefree, but free.

5

L ate September is a slow burn of leaves and earth and rain. Sun during the day, but night's razor-sharp premonition of ice and snow and short days and endless nights slices Laine without her feeling it.

Laine rises before her roommate, moves quietly in the blue mornings. The sunrise starts white, and blooms into pink tangerine, sending vines of gold into Laine's center, pulling her up. Most students wake by alarm or a sense of urgency or a roommate's voice, but Laine always wakes in this elementary way.

Nikki sleeps in unruly pleasure, legs kicked over sheets, mouth open, dreams spilling like drool. There's a warm, milky, sweet sleep smell that makes Laine sick. She sneaks away like a thief except she hasn't taken anything. If pressed, she can't say why, but she feels desperate to get out of the room. Just being in the room sometimes makes Laine feel guilty. It's as if Nikki walks around naked and no one wants to tell her, or as if she's trailing ten feet of toilet paper stuck to her heel.

And so Nikki wakes alone and has to find a breakfast partner. She starts out disoriented, figures out who she is, and wonders how she'll make it through the day. It's been two weeks, and it hasn't gotten easier, and Nikki tries not to panic or give up, swinging in the in-between. She consults the mirror, dabs on gloss, flicks hair, but really she's looking to see if her identity has re-crystallized, if the fire's back in her honey eyes, *if I've become a prep school student yet.* And there, in the glass, is a wan, amorphous face looking to *her* for answers.

Today Nikki gets into the shower after Dawn, who left the bathroom stinking of diarrhea, and minutes later is startled by a rap on the stall door. Dawn's hand fishes under the door: "Can you hand me that little setup there I forgot?"

Nikki looks down at a "strawberry flavor" douche in the corner. *Are you effing kidding me? Why don't I just brush my teeth with your vibrator?* She uses a washcloth to transfer the item.

Once dressed, she peeks in the hall for an escort to the special performance required this morning. Aya pulls hot water from the cooler into a mug. Black bob shiny, zebra robe transparent, she winks one lavender eyelid but saunters past, tea bag tag fluttering. Charlotte runs down the hall, cream and tan hounds tooth coat flapping, face old-fashioned and beautiful like a cameo, and fingers hiding the pearly scar of a harelip.

Then the gangly girl pokes her head from her room, like a mouse out of the wall. Parker was in Nikki's orientation group, but kept to herself then and ever since has refused to give Nikki the time of day. Anytime Nikki's tried to connect, Parker skitters away. Her blouse is a puffy Laura Ingalls Wilder number, her skirt is patchwork. Waist-length hair swings. She wears dark-framed glasses.

"You going to the thing at the auditorium?" Nikki asks.

"I'm just, you know, I don't know. Sorry."

"Why are you sorry?" Nikki says.

"No, I mean, I'm going."

"I dig your skirt, it almost looks homemade."

"Well, yeah. I did make it."

"Oh. Wow. So then . . . should we go?"

"Of course! Right."

Am I so repellant that these people can't talk to me? What is the goddamn story?

They walk in the damp morning, Nikki smarting with anger or pride, trying to bear the silence. The landscape is dark and ruffled, white mist clinging, the sky low.

Parker looks behind her as though she thinks she's being followed, then checks her bag to see what she forgot. In between, she tucks hair behind her ear. *Christ,* Nikki thinks, *it's okay to walk with me across the freaking campus.* Nikki asks about her leather cuff, trying again to break the ice.

Parker holds out her arm; the band's stenciled RISK. "Yeah. My mom went to Berkeley. She was all about, like, Gloria Steinem and solar power and transcendental meditation. You know."

"I don't know, but whatever. Was that her book bag?" Nikki asks.

Parker holds up the battered schoolbag. "My dad's, while he was getting his Ph.D. He knew I loved it, so he gave it to me when they dropped me off here. I'm, like, way attached to these things because I'm having some trouble adjusting, I guess. I just miss home a bit." Parker clutches at her bag, and Nikki sees her long white fingers tremble.

Oh my God, she's a wreck.

Nikki also notices, as they confront the building's bright lights, Parker's red eyes. She links her arm through Parker's, and although the gangly girl with the smell of violets and the horn-rim glasses jumps, she pulls Nikki tight and they enter the golden-lit room.

Laine is nested into a clutch of Lower- and Upper-form girls when Nikki and Parker enter, and her big eyes track them to a seat in the back. *Interesting. Instant best friends, like*

microwave oatmeal. Laine feels relief, and something like surprise—not jealousy, it couldn't be that. Nikki hasn't managed to wrangle anyone till today. Laine is already at the
center of a crew. This happens sometimes, the accretion of
a social hive around one sturdily pedigreed person—even if
that person does nothing to invite the crowd, even if that
person barely interacts with the hangers-on.

The special occasion is a documentary made by a
Wellington alum, who is sitting now in a leather armchair
on stage below the screen. He'd filmed endangered lynxes
making their secretive ways through the snow, and everyone in the big room is hushed.

At one point Laine twists to check the twosome, and
light from the projection is sliding across their faces, both
of them entranced. Laine surveys the girls she's with, and
decides she's the only one lost on the exterior of the film,
not permitted inside. And she's on the outside of her own
in-crowd. *What's new.*

This summer Laine sometimes had the sensation while
playing tennis that she was playing and also sitting on the
bench in rich shade, waiting her turn. And in a way, she
remembers this sensation now but doesn't relate it to her
own life, as if the memory belonged to someone else.
That's Laine: a hundred feet away from herself at all times.

Laine is a bundle of nerves today, her throat rejecting food.

But she can't play right without fuel, and works it in. Before heading to the pivotal practice, Laine sneaks a moment in her room, lies on the floor to stretch but it's really to soak the sunspot like a cat. She's an animal seeking consolation, strength. She copes with stress by circumnavigating emotions and going straight to the body.

Walking to the fields she frets. After two weeks of practice, this is the first scrimmage, an indication of how Miss H is thinking about lines. Laine *must* make first line. First-liners make Futures (the Olympic development team and an acknowledged scoutfest), and girls on Futures make Ivies. Miss H's favorite first-liners make Ivies on grants and big financial aid packages: basically full rides. Laine wants a full ride so neither her father nor her stepfather will pay a dime—the ultimate *no, thank you.*

The path is perforated by cleat tines. The school builds itself into her as she crosses the yards every day, staining her with history. The Watkins Science Building was refurbished during the Cold War when trustees pointed to science as salvation. The Sasson Observatory was funded by the estate of a dreamy, sickly alum who died in 1938 in a Cambodian opium den, a man so enchanted by the moon and stars that he willed the contraption to the school. The Manchester-Dublins Art Museum & Art Wing were a late-1980s project, and a daily job for the school PR team—the Manchesters were rumored to own more art stolen by Nazis than any family in the United States. When Sylvia Manchester donated a Picasso sketch to the school, a *New York Times* reporter got a whiff of the story and the transaction was shut down.

"Hey," two guys call, gym bags over big shoulders, and she waves back, grinning in embarrassment, not knowing them and startled out of solitude. The taller guy catches a yellow leaf spiraling from a tree.

Someone else runs to catch up to her from behind; she hears his breath. It's Chase. He throws his hands into his pockets and slows down. Hair mussed by the wind, tie thrown over his shoulder.

"Hey there, Laine," he drawls, catching his breath.

"Hi," she says, already tongue-tied.

"You're heading to practice, I guess."

"Yeah . . ." She racks her brain. "And you are too?"

"Yup. Heading to practice."

"Me too," Laine says, then goes scarlet. "Field hockey." Turns purple now.

"Right, we discussed that at the picnic, I think. I mean, I'm not sure, I think we did."

When they part ways at the mouth of the gym, both are relieved. Laine watches him vanish into Slattery Gym, his long hair and grave stride somehow reminiscent of sixties students, of old-fashioned idealism.

The indoor athletic facility, which she approaches now,

truly contains both past and future. If Laine breathes deeply, she can lose herself in it. The outer chambers—from the seven squash courts to the Olympic pools to the weight rooms—are glass-walled, lofty, dazzling, hi-tech spaces. But the structure's hub is a subterranean chronicle of Wellington's beginning. Underground there are preserved dank gyms where boys once wrestled in woolen leotards, the rifle range where they prepared for World War II, the Cage where Tommy has distributed gear for thirty-one years, and the Trainers Room. *This is where my dreams begin.*

The Trainers Room is white-tiled like an antique steam room. Smells like menthol, sweaty pads, gauze, soil on cleats. Gretchen Briggs is on the table getting her knee taped, talking to Brett, who relaxes his hamstring in the hot whirlpool.

"Who's next, nowah? Is it you?" Pug, the short, dog-faced trainer gestures with bulky arms at Laine. She hops onto the table. Pug is beloved by athletes for the care he takes of joints, wounds, egos. He used to box, thus the crushed nose, and his Maine accent is so wicked Laine asks him to repeat himself.

"Theyah?" he asks, pressing his thumb on her swollen ankle.

"Yikes, yes, right there," Laine says.

He rubs icy cream into her skin, wraps it with padding, tapes it; she's prone to tendonitis. But Pug takes his position further than just this physical nurturing, into the realm of the Socratic trainer, like the spiritual mentor for wrestlers of yore. Pug carries on a tradition of mysticism in sport, of profound statements, of moral intimacy in athletics.

"You're kind of Zen, ain't you tigah?" he says now.

"What?"

"You're a hahd nut to crack. You got a deep centah." He thuds his chest to demonstrate.

Miss Hartford is standing over the procedure now, arms crossed and legs apart, defiant and maternal at the same time. "We're pumped to have this player, Pug."

When Miss H talks to her, Laine is identified—to the PG soccer players from Brazil, the tattooed football player, the Harlem track star—as a *player*.

Laine and Miss H walk, and Laine carries the canvas bag of balls. As coach and athlete, they're past courting, but still not in love. Miss H asks how Laine found this summer's training letters, and Laine says they were *great*. Especially sprint mechanics, and eating *after* practice, how to store up glycogen in muscles. As they come over the hill, they stop talking: Four fields are laid end to end to make one green estate, lines straight and white, nets aligned, girls rolling balls between stunted, dowdy ends of sticks or tapping the ball forward in sprints.

This is where I live. Laine and Miss H are made of the same material. They step out of the messy world and onto this field where running burns away impurities, leaving them clean and hard. Making them real again. The coach smiles at the player, and the player smiles back.

On the field, Miss H is the quintessential coach, with a military style of favoring, chiding, punishing, rewarding. Her dark corn-yellow hair is bluntly cut and shining. She has the face of a teenager that has aged but not coalesced into the face of a woman. But her body has prowess. Her muscles dense with years of practice, defeat, victory, discipline, devotion. No one would mistake her for a player.

They've been doing 2 V 2 drills for about twenty minutes when Miss H blows her whistle, holding out green pinnies. She calls them into a circle. *Come on, start me,* Laine thinks. Clouds rush in a cool wind that tousles ponytails and the edges of Umbros, rifling the pages on Miss H's clipboard. The girls squint, wait.

Miss H holds her hair back with one hand off her forehead. "Players. Remember what I wrote in your letters. Remember *flow.* You cannot flow if you are not *centered.* You can't play like a winner if you are trying to win. You are not trying to win. You are trying to play at your hundred-twenty-percent in *this moment.* Don't look two miles down the road. Don't think two minutes ahead. You are here, now.

"What happens if you make a mistake?" she quizzes.

Schuyler, captain, answers: "Train your mind back out,

to the moment."

Miss H asks them what tool reclaims their center.

"Breathing," two girls say.

Miss H looks at her sheets, at their hieroglyphics, secrets, coded plays. "All right."

Everyone waits in the chilly breeze, no one even daring to un-Velcro a glove to make it tighter. The long field waits. *I'm breathing*, Laine thinks.

"Okay, offense playing thataway," Miss H points down field. "Paige, Schuyler, Rory, Laine . . ."

Laine's ecstatically lined up against MK at center, which means she's being considered for first line. Mary-Katherine, the returning starter with a taste for vintage 501s and Copenhagen snuff, is circled in most Facebooks with a heart. Her laugh is easy, and she's always throwing an arm around people, telling a story in a low voice that makes them laugh with her. If Schuyler rules the straight alpha table, MK reigns over the deviant alpha table. Normally girls who dip keep it secret, but MK flaunts it. Maybe it's her Southern accent or her resemblance to Kate Hudson, but guys practically drool over her dip spit. It's rumored she and her boyfriend swap chews when they make out.

They stand in position now, crouching slightly, under the gray sky. The ball, white like bone, is thrown between their sticks. Laine goes in, sticks clack, but MK maneuvers with famous stick control, almost impaling the ball like fruit on a spike. MK takes it downfield but Laine hasn't given up as many do with MK, and runs tightly around— MK doesn't even realize her pass to Kiersten could be blocked. In fact she's so shocked she stops running, a cardinal sin on Miss H's field.

Whistle. "MK, you run through it, you circle around, use the energy. Stopping and turning loses all momentum. Go offense to D in a heartbeat. Come on."

"Sorry, Miss H," she says, and then under her breath, to Laine: "Dang, girl, you blindsided me!"

Laine sees that MK's tiny chip in one front tooth makes her prettier in some reckless way. She nods, and they take positions for a free hit.

After scrimmaging, the girls shine in the darkening afternoon, faces glowing with heat. Shirts shiver with their panting. Miss H is lining up sawhorses and everyone gapes. *Hurdles.*

Miss H doesn't even smile. "Hurdles, players. Train like you play. Remember, pain is weakness leaving the body."

The girls sprint, jumping sawhorses, legs dying, food rising. Some girls are bright red. They run Suicides after, even though many barely made it through hurdles, and Miss H yells one of her mantras: "Run *crisp*, players, run cuh-risp. Economy, not just speed. Crisp."

I run crisp.

It's then Laine remembers last night's dream. Across a

night field, she raced on Penelope's white back, raising dirt in clouds. The way the earth pounded under the hooves hurt as it reverberated through Laine's body, but then her own body melded with the horse. They became one animal, and it rode faster and harder than she ever did before, and the pain turned to a kind of euphoria.

6

Nikki stands at the mouth of the dining hall. Lunch is the frontlines. It's kill or be killed. Breakfast, you can grab something and run, or it's *almost* socially acceptable to sit alone and scarf Cheerios. Dinner, everyone rolls in with teammates. But lunch. *Effing lunch.* It's dense, the shortest meal, and it's a show.

It's fight or flight. Walk into the hall, wooden chandeliers dimly lighting the pale afternoon. Use your best laissez-faire strut. You slowly work your way down the hot buffet, holding your chipped plate out to hostile, gap-toothed locals and let them pile food on it. Get some milk, stalling, from the huge metal udderlike contraptions that flank the hot buffet. If you still can't identify with peripheral vision a place to sit, make a fruit cup at the cold buffet. After the fruit cup, that's it. Time to turn and walk into the fray.

Today Nikki loads up with two fruit cups, *if that says anything,* and beelines to Chase's table, which is crowded but has one open spot. These guys are fickle, sometimes loving her, sometimes not. As she nears, the boys make quick eye contact with one another. *Do not,* she begs in her mind. *Do not do this to me.*

Chase is slouching, as always, with chocolate milk. The kid barely consumes food. He looks at her apologetically. "I'm sorry, Nik, that's Burns's seat; he's on his way."

Noah sings in a Gregorian chant since he's just come from Medieval Music class: "Get thee to another table, Nicole, go sit thyself there with thy other gender-folks."

"Ha, ha, so funny," Nikki says, her brain already imploding with panic. *How to save face, sit down anyway, and tell them to fuck off? Or keep walking as if I wasn't going to sit there? Panic. Paralysis. Panic.*

Somehow she finds herself sitting at the next table, with Mi-long and Dawn, blinded by humiliation and anxiety. She smiles weakly at the two girls, who don't want her either, and picks the purple grapes from her fruit cups.

It wouldn't have been so horrible if Chase didn't clear Laine a place two minutes later. Chase is careful not to look back in Nikki's direction. *Shows he knows.*

But Laine is as uncomfortable at the table as Nikki is *not* at the table. When Chase asks about her baked potato and energy gel and V-8, and she explains glycogen stores in the muscle, the table is freaked out. They go quiet. *Just keep your mouth shut, Laine. Smile, eat, and give them a laugh every so often.*

Burns is a red-cheeked, eighty-pound, insolent legacy, stupid in most ways and genius in a few, doomed or charmed to float in a limbo of privilege his whole life.

He points a fork at Laine. "You look like, like eight years old, you know? But you sound like you've been smoking and, like, swilling whiskey for forty years."

The table guffaws at him, although Laine can't be sure it's not at her. She has no finesse in analyzing this stuff.

"Okay, Burns?" Chase drawls, not sitting up from his slouch. "Who the hell are *you?*"

"Yeah, you short little bastard. You're one to talk," Noah jumps on.

"I mean you've got no *style*, Burns. Look at your necktie. It looks like someone wiped their ass with it. Who dresses you, Johnny Drama?" Chase drawls.

As Burns examines his dirty tie (a pheasant embroidered on tobacco brown silk), Greg says: "Have you met Burns's webcam girlfriend? She's an eleven-year-old from somewhere—"

Burns pipes up. "Murta's Dutch, and she's twelve, thank you very much. And I got her to finger her anus on IM last night."

Greg spits his juice back into his cup. "Jesus CHRIST, we're eating."

"She's a spicy little number. Says she can barely handle my girth."

"No shit, huh?" Chase says. "Have another lunch break sess today, tiger? You got to get off the Wite-Out, kid. By the way, the communal showers aren't doing you any favors with that line of bullshit."

Greg turns to Laine. "Burns here comes into Bio 3 yesterday with white on his sideburns from huffing into a Ziploc bag. Smart, right?"

"Oh yeah?" Laine says. "That's funny."

Chase adds, "In his own way, he's a mastermind. Take that horse-betting scheme last week; it financed a month's worth of bud and handles for the floor."

Burns asks Laine if he can have her V8. Laine pushes it to him, laughing, glad the guys are happier talking *for* her than with her. Relieves her of the stress of flirting—*which some girls were born to do, and some, like me, were born to mangle.*

As Nikki's leaving, Parker arrives—and sees Laine's head bowed at the table of doting guys. Nikki and Parker look at each other, Parker surmising the situation, shaking her head.

Nikki tells her she wishes she could save her, there being no one to sit with in this shift either.

"I wish you could too," Parker says. "This isn't really

working for me."

This is what they say. If they walk into dinner and don't like the food, they say *this isn't really working for me.* One of them finds the other about to meltdown, *this isn't really working for me. Are we going to make it through this place? I dunno. Cuz this really isn't working for me.*

"Where you headed?" Parker asks, stalling.

"Psych. To discuss 'the human behavior of individuals when cornered into groups.'"

"You could learn more if you stayed here."

Lying on the sheets that have absorbed the grime of stress and sadness of her first couple weeks, Nikki falls into her "Bounce Reverie."

She envisions the laundry room at home, late afternoon, gold light streaking in with force, coming sideways. The checkerboard floor, the machines rumbling. And Sharon pulls sheets from the dryer, their hot fragrance potent as baking bread to a hungry man—and that light shines through the fabric as she folds, and folds again.

A new mound of wet clothes is moved from washer to dryer, and this, here, this moment is the most delicate of all: Sharon's French manicure winks as her fingers take hold of a sheet of Bounce, and slowly—Nikki slows it down in this daydream to a devout pace—the page of fabric softener is extracted from the box, and it too catches the light, its fiber almost phosphorescent, and it shines before it is tossed into the dark machine.

Nikki sleeps.

By the time Laine's stepdad finally get through, phone hours are almost over so they have only a few minutes to talk. They rush through basics.

"Any favorite teachers yet?"

"Um, Ballast most likely. English. Really upbeat, on target." Laine says this because everyone loves him, but she never knows what Ballast is talking about. Her classes are all more difficult than she expected. At home, the teachers had all known her since kindergarten, and coached her through rough spots.

"And your roommate, you two getting along?"

"Absolutely." Nikki looks up from her own desk as if she knows she's the subject.

"Laine, I wish I got you earlier, there's a number of things I'd love to know about. Call me and your mother tomorrow if you get the chance, would you?"

Laine's scrambled when she gets off the phone. She likes and respects Philip, even though circumstances have made it hard to bond. He's the rare event of a man born so privileged he would have been running companies no matter what, unless he was a complete disaster—but is naturally wise, strong, and brilliant, and would have made it exactly as far as he has even without a leg up. When they talk, he asks questions and wants to know answers. He listens. She just can't ever be sure he *wants* another daughter. He reminds her of an esteemed professor who lets a student into a full class, or a congressman who takes an earnest intern even though the last thing he needs is another intern.

His other kids already did prep school, and then college. They all look exactly like him. But I don't have his eyes, his pigeon toes, his photographic memory. His heart isn't in me.

Saturday evening, electric twilight falling among trees, Nikki knocks on Parker's door, as prearranged.

"Yo," Nik says. "What's up, girl?"

"Hi there." Parker is cross-legged on her bed, sewing. Parker's always got a project, like drying tangerine peels on the radiator to smoke or making a flip book of a man being hanged.

"What you got?" Nikki asks, sprawling over the chair.

Parker holds up a vintage handkerchief she's embroidering with little black skull-and-crossbones emblems.

"Dude, what in the *hell* is that, Park?"

"It's a vintage handkerchief embroidered with little black skull-and-crossbones emblems."

"Well, I can kind of see that for myself, honey. What are you going to do, stuff them in Christmas stockings for your family?"

Parker suddenly looks up, pushes her glasses. "That's not a bad idea."

Nikki laughs, twirls on the chair. Neither girl would admit it, but each is hopeful about tonight's dance. Two pictures have been taped up near Parker's bed, and Nikki stops twirling to peer at them. "Who's this?"

Parker looks over, needle suspended above cloth. "That's Chet Baker on the left, and the other picture is Joey Ramone."

"These are your boyzzzz?"

Parker gets pink. "I guess."

"The one on the right is fucking ugly, no offense. You ever write them letters?"

"Well. They're both dead, so no."

"You're in love with two dead guys?"

Parker shrugs.

Nikki laughs raucously. "Don't you think that hurts your chances a little bit?"

Schuyler and Laine make noise in the hall coming back from practice.

"I wonder if she's going to the dance," Nikki says.

"You mean your roommate? I gotta say, Nik. You are kind of obsessed."

Nikki plays with Parker's stapler. She looks pissed at first. "You think I like her? You think I want her to pet my bunny?"

Parker looks confused, then turns scarlet.

"I want her to click my mouse?" Nikki taunts.

"Gross!" Parker says, which is strong language, having never been allowed to curse by her homeschooling, holistic father.

"I'm kidding. Damn, you are effing sensitive." She hesitates. "I dunno."

"You don't know what?"

"I guess I imagined, I dunno. That I'd be friends with my roommate. Like, good friends. And meanwhile, she can barely be in the same room as me. It's twisted, you know? Hey, Betsy Ross, get ready, we gotta get over there. We gots to see and be seen."

Nikki stretches on the bed as Parker gets up to brush her hair. "I mean, what *is* Laine's deal? She's effing spooky! Those big eyes. I'm like, *Hello, are you there?*"

Parker's changing (crouching behind the desk) into a mustard-yellow dress with macramé belt and brown cowboy boots.

"Where on earth did you find that outfit?" Nikki takes a break to ask.

"Umm, thrift stores in Quebec, and from my aunt's attic."

"Jesus."

"I don't know what to tell you, Nik. I think Laine's a snob, to be honest. I think she's a rich bitch."

Nikki's never heard Parker so negative. "Well, how do you really feel?" she jokes, not sure why she feels protective.

"I'm sorry. I am, it's mean. But I wouldn't waste my time on her. There's nothing there."

Saturday nights at Wellington bear an eerie resemblance to nights at senior citizen centers. Early Bird Special in the dining hall. A movie. A dance in the gym. And a wildly extended curfew of—brace yourself!—eleven o'clock.

The girls catch the tail end of *American Pie,* and then surge with the crowd, hopped up on darkness and low expectations, out the banging doors of the auditorium. Soda cans of dip spit and coffee cups with Beam and Coke spill in the aisles.

Fluorescent light cascades through gym windows as they approach en masse up the lamplit path. From the outside, the athletic center looks like a colony on Mars, tubular and gigantic, glowing with electricity. Inside, teak furniture surrounds a flat-screen television in the Coaches Corner. A Wellington emblem is carved into the lobby's hardwood floor. Pennants hang from iron rafters.

The basketball gym has been transformed into a wannabe rave. Through the smoke machine's haze, strobe lights blink.

"This looks cheesy as shit." Nikki snickers almost bitterly.

Parker looks at Nikki, in low-slung jeans with pink thong showing, Steve Madden boots, and a black hoodie. "I guess so," Parker agrees.

They walk through the crowd. Nikki feels stares, and her body lights up like a siren. The Black Eyed Peas bump in the foggy dark. Most girls spent the early evening studying their Face books as if memorizing baseball cards. The guys hail from all corners of the globe, from royal estates and urban projects. By staring at these photos with hometown addresses, studying them harder than any logarithm or chemical equation, girls feel somehow armed to conquer.

A disco ball spangles all those faces now.

"See that blond kid over there? He's the one from Florida I showed you," Nikki says.

"Uh-huh," Parker says under her breath, as if the guy could hear Nikki across the crowd.

Nikki has picked the most public school kid in the room, with a basketball jersey and bleached bangs. She doesn't understand yet that the hierarchy of boys is backward. The slouchers, the kids with scuffed bucks, greasy hair, and easy laughs: Those are the studs here. She's never been without a boyfriend or at least a crush, a conquest, but she hasn't figured out the landscape yet.

Upper-form white guys grind younger girls with little success. The black and Latino crowd take a section of floor and don't look at the white crowd. Greg moves through the cliques, though, flicking dirt off his shoulder. Nikki gets his attention, knees bent, hands in position on her thighs.

"You about to get it now." Greg laughs.

She laughs, plays along, adrenaline rising like mercury.

Most of the white girls avoid dancing or can't dance. They sing along like sorority sisters, but can't hear the beat. Out of the corner of her eye Nikki catches Laine doing the Humpty-Hump with Schuyler. Limping with one leg, spinning with the other. *I bet she loves that everyone sees her hanging with Senior girls. We're all so impressed.*

The music cuts, everyone stops. The deejay throws on Shakedown Street, and from the margins come sideburned, long-haired kids in overalls. Kids point and clap. The wookies finally get to dance. It's white-man's-overbite and noodling, with Molly-Ringwald-in-*The-Breakfast-Club* thrown in.

"Hey, Nik?" Parker taps Nikki eventually, stealing her attention from the rain dance. "I think I'm going to head."

"Parker, you can't leave!" Nikki begs; then in a covert mutter: "Those guys are about to come over here."

"Nikki, honestly, I'm so not into this tonight."

Seth Walters's dark hair hangs down to his eyes. He saunters up, hands in his pockets, slouching like a tough guy. His friend Diego trails him. Nikki grabs Parker's sleeve and hisses to stay. *It's the guy from the raft. Interesting.*

"Hey, what's your name?" Seth is confident, but not

cocky. He isn't laughing with his friends or smiling sheepishly at her. He comes off natural.

Nikki starts to do her giggly thing that makes guys comfortable, but realizes halfway in that he's not interested. *Okay.* "I'm Nikki. This is Parker."

As Diego reaches to shake Parker's hand, Parker walks backward. They all stare as she says: "I'm sorry, I was just. I'm tired, I have to head back. Nik, see you tomorrow. Okay, bye . . ." And then runs. Nikki suddenly understands that Parker wasn't going home despite the fact that guys were coming to talk to them, but because of it.

Diego laughs sarcastically. "Three's a crowd, bro. I'm out." They slap hands in a desultory way and part. Nikki is left with this dark horse whose shiny black hair hangs perpetually across one eye, who manages to make biting his nails look sexy.

"So you like it here or what?" he says, smiling in a hopeful, almost apologetic way. "It's a little strange, but if you figure out how to deal—it's a decent time."

Nikki looks across the dance floor to a few teachers staring back. *Is it because I'm talking to a guy? Oh, God. They already hate me.*

Seth looks. "Don't mind them. They're always after me. I've been asked to leave twice, but I just can't get *enough* of this shithole."

Nikki feels more weight than just the teachers' gazes,

and notices Schuyler staring, too. *That girl can't get enough of me.* "Has that girl Schuyler gotten laid this year?"

Seth grins and Nikki catches a whiff of gin. "I like it here," she adds, shrugging. "I already met some cool people, I guess. I'm sure it gets better."

"Seems like you have good kids in your class. You know Chase, right? Stick with him, he's a funny dude. I knew his brother real well. Chase is a little comatose tonight, but it happens to everyone at first. No shortage of smoke during the first few weeks at school. Come Christmas time, we'll be scraping every bowl in the dorm."

Seth leans back so Nikki can see Chase: eyes slits, hand clutching a bag of Sour Cream & Onion chips. He gives a quick wave and she sees crumbs on his face and powder on fingertips.

"Classic!" Nikki says, then shouts to Chase, "What's up, Kumar?"

Chase winks.

Finally the dance is clearing out, but one European kid is going hard. His Italian football shirt sweaty, pale jeans clinging to his thighs. He's lost in techno bliss. A crowd circles. Jorgen pumps his fists, excited people are watching. He pumps harder, shouting to the crowd, "Go, go, go!"

The Senior girl dancing with him tries to smile.

Timothy Pickford is one of the Seniors witnessing Jorgen seal his fate.

"Would you look at this douche?" he asks no one in particular. "This is glorious."

Three years prior Tim had cemented his own name by humping a prepubescent girl from Nebraska during his orientation dance. To this day he's known as "Standards," and is a Wellington casualty trying desperately now to pass on the crown.

Nikki can feel Seth watching her. This guy is growing on her, fast; he isn't like anyone she's known with his hopeless eyes and stringy hair, the mean shrug of his shoulders. He's not too big, about 5'10", but his shoulders are broad and they slope. He yawns, and then stretches, which pulls up his T-shirt. His stomach, right above his boxers' waistband, is hard and white as marble. Nikki starts to feel dizzy.

"I'm going to head," she says. *Tell me not to go, come with me, take my hand, make me stay.*

"Let me walk you back?" He smiles and pushes his bangs out of his eyes.

Of course I'll let you. But she says: "I think I'll manage on my own."

"Oh, c'mon, you shouldn't walk in the dark alone. We'll go smoke a butt on the way."

There you go. Nikki lets herself swoon and land in that place a girl sometimes finds when a man puts his heavy arm across her shoulders—the other world.

They walk along the woods, the stars brutally sharp in the cold sky. They're startled by a crash of branches and underbrush—a deer, invisible in the night, hurls itself away from the pair into the heart of the woods.

"This is a premium spot," Seth tells her, ushering her into a small garage.

Antique groundskeeping machinery shines dully in night shadows. These retired machines rust in here; the working garage is behind the science building. Seth lights two cigarettes, jaw shining in the Bic's flame as he tilts his head. Nikki acts calm but her body is flickering. As he leans against a tractor and talks about his own first year, she concentrates on smoking, ashing, and being still.

"You know, I grew up in Santa Barbara. I showed up here wearing Oakleys and a Hurley T-shirt and everyone looked at me like I was insane. I might as well have been wearing a goddamn NASA space suit. Four years later, and look at me. I got my bucks, I got my Skoal. We all fade, my friend. For better or worse."

"I don't know what the *hell* bucks are, but there's no way I'm wearing them," Nikki says and Seth laughs. She's encouraged: "No khaki, no headbands, no red corduroy motherloving jumpers with effing white *turtlenecks*. Come on, ladies, this is not first grade."

"I especially like the way guys wear jackets too small or whatever." Seth gestures and his cigarette makes red rings in the dark. "Like if your clothes fit you're a snob. Your shit should be falling apart, the hem undone 'cause it's, like, your great-uncle's Brooks Brothers herringbone whatever. You know?"

When Nikki laughs, her head ruffles a sheaf of pages nailed to the wall, and she turns.

"You should check this out," Seth says, clenching his butt between teeth and holding the lighter to the papers. "People, like, tacked all this shit up here, over time."

"What is it?"

"Mnn," he says, and takes a drag with no hands, blows smoke through teeth. "It's the Tripped-and-Fell list, torn from yearbooks. The kids who didn't make it. Got kicked out or asked to leave, not invited back one year—all three things very different, FYI. Or they just left, couldn't take it. Went AWOL."

Nikki reads names as his lighter skims. "Crap, that's a lot of names."

"Yeah, each list here is one year."

"WHAT? That's like thirty people out of that class! Out of a hundred fifty?"

"Yeah, they fill in as they go along. Happens everywhere, but especially at a No Second Chance school like Wellington."

"Shit, I never thought it was such a big deal."

"Yeah, they don't brag about it in the Admissions

office." Seth lets the pages fall, the light go out.

The list of names somehow enhances Nik's long, raw, last drag. They twist their smokes on the oily floor, and he takes her hand to cross the night fields. Seth walks her all the way back, and she leans in to him as they stand guarded by willow trees behind Lancaster. She isn't sure why, but she feels close to him, even if he's not completely making sense, even if he's weaving slightly and might not remember exactly what they talked about tomorrow.

She goes to kiss his lips, but he takes her heart-shaped face in his hands and kisses her forehead. Then he walks away, backward, not quite sure on his feet. But suave, his bare arms cold in the night, black hair over one eye, hands in pockets. A tough guy.

"G'night," she says.

You might not pick him out of a crowd, but you might. He's that guy. And the longer he's near you, the more you'll start to realize what you got. He moves slow but with a margin for yawning, stretching, rubbing his own hard stomach. He's got the ease of a guy who grew up skating or snowboarding or hiking. He's got wilderness. Out of nowhere, he's mine. And screw all y'all, cuz you got no one.

. . .

Laine walks back alone. *What a lame night,* she thinks with more resentment than she can understand. Hung out in the corner with other field hockey girls. That was it. Beginning and end. *Gee, how exciting.* She kicks an acorn and it rattles into the shadows.

"Hey, don't do that," someone says.

She squints, and there outside Appleby a skinny faculty kid, a fac-brat, stares with menacing friendliness, his face further torqued by lamplight. He holds his bike up and asks her name.

"Laine." She walks faster, uncomfortable making small talk, even with kids.

"Mine's Edgar," he says, his tone chastising her for not asking.

"Sorry," she mumbles.

"Did you go to the dance?" he says, eyes aglow in the night.

"Yeah, it was stupid." *Why on earth am I having this conversation?*

"Yeah," he says quietly, agreeing or disconnecting, she's not sure. He clumsily gets on his bike, rides circles in the lamp's gold circumference.

What a weird childhood. With hundreds of temporary siblings, who never collectively get older and never get younger.

He calls as she nears Lancaster: "You know it's rude not to say good night."

She glares at his silhouette. She can't bring herself to say good night.

Nikki floats up the stairs. She slips into their room just before curfew. A tree branch trembles in moonlight on their floor. Nikki slides into bed, pulls the sheets around her body.

She whispers: "Are you asleep?"

"Kind of," Laine says, after turning away.

"Did you leave the dance early?"

"Practice was brutal."

"Was it?" Nikki says hoarsely, trying to maximize this exchange. She feels good, like this place might start hard but get better. "You're on Varsity, right?"

Laine grunts.

Nikki asks if she knows Seth. "He walked me home. He's effing *beautiful*, don't you think?"

Laine rolls over again.

"Shit, I've got Bombay Sapphire on my lips. I feel drunk and I didn't even drink."

Laine is silent a moment. Then: "No offense," she says, her voice muffled. "But I'm tired, and whatever. Besides, don't you think it's kinda early to be working the campus?"

7

ield hockey has three teams: Varsity, JV, and Thirds. From Varsity, a few girls ride field hockey careers to the college of their dreams. Girls from JV can move up to Varsity if they have natural ability and train hard.

Girls on Thirds are hopeless.

Today, Thirds is more hysterical than usual, possibly because a storm is coming. Where Varsity is sleek and fearless, Thirds is dumpy or gangly, with low morale and delinquent undertones. Girls brave prickly undergrowth to retrieve balls, scraping thighs on thorns. Parker and Nikki start a water bottle fight between drills, squirting cold water in arcs. Nikki sees Laine miss a goal on the far field, and imitates Laine's chagrin. Parker laughs.

"What, you don't like your girlfriend anymore?"

Parker asks.

Nikki laughs, looking away. "Nah. I think you're right, she's a bitch."

The sky is mottled peach and gray, radiant. The trees are stark and dense. Walnuts fall and girls knock them with their sticks back into the woods between sprints.

Parker and Nikki linger after practice, dillydallying, letting the team start up to the locker room. Parker puts on her ratty white fur jacket over shorts and a T-shirt, and the girls head into the woods. Parker hand-rolls cigarettes for them. With shin guards on and her knobbed stick over her shoulder, walking through a grove of ferns, she looks like a child lost from civilization.

Parker's from Canada, and to Nikki she might as well be from Saturn. Each time Nikki thinks she knows the girl, Parker's opposite. Nikki imagined her to be vegetarian, but no, she goes bow-and-arrow deer hunting with her dad. She took her for a nonsmoker, but Parker can roll a fine twist with her eyes closed and one hand tied behind her back.

"What the fuck are we doing?" Nikki asks, touching her stick's end to some moss on a tree.

"Smoking in the woods." Parker strikes a match and lights the twists of paper.

"I'm aware. I mean, what are we doing playing this retarded game?" Nikki takes hers, inhales carefully, picks tobacco off her tongue. "It's not really working for me."

The air in the woods is rich, and holds their words as if they were precious.

Parker's now playing with her Walkman. She might be the only person in the world who still listens to tapes.

"What you got?" Nikki asks.

They each walk with one speaker in one ear, attached like Siamese twins by the cord. Guitars crash and squeal.

"What *is* this?"

"Dead Kennedys."

"What's wrong with, like, Mariah Carey or something?"

"Who?"

Birds make shadows in the tall canopy, fluttering, diving, crying.

"I don't know," Nikki says. "I don't know why we're obeying the status quo so easy, you know? Isn't there something else we could do? I suck at field hockey."

Parker looks as though she's about to comfort Nikki. "You do suck."

"Omygod, eff you!" Nikki shoves her.

"It's cool, I do too," Parker says, fending Nikki off and laughing. "Not as much as you, of course. But honestly, why *are* we playing this stupid game?"

"Because it seemed like the thing to do."

"This is the beginning of the end! We're acting like sheep, Nik. We'll be wearing cashmere twin sets next."

"For real. This is serious."

"Being here, it's like loving someone who's a little crazy. You just start to believe in their lunatic rules and stuff. But you're not doing anyone any favors by going along with the madness."

Nikki doesn't press it, but it seems Parker has some experience with this.

They ash on the damp floor of the forest, trudge through mist past lichen-painted trees.

Parker turns off the Walkman and faces her friend. "Okay, let's figure out Plan B. Right?"

Nikki smiles. "No more Thirds for us. I'm on it."

The locker room buzzes. Both JV and Thirds field hockey shower while Girls Track & Field trickle in. Parker changes in a bathroom stall, refusing to get into communal showers. Nikki lathers in her private Dove commercial. As girls rinse shampoo or shave legs, their bodies are inventoried by peers—and will be leaked to the general population. A Prep with a Brazilian bikini wax is notorious overnight, while a Lower-form with an aberrant trail of hair down her back is without a Christmas Formal date.

Nikki now rubs lotion into her skin at her locker. She asks Parker if she showered.

Parker pouts at the situation. "This looks like a health spa in Warsaw or something."

"Is that a no?"

Parker's changed into a long Irish knit sweater, black stovepipe pants, and motorcycle boots.

"You look like some kind of punk fisherman," Nikki says.

Parker glances at herself, then looks up, pleased. "Thank you," she says, almost coyly.

The Varsity team arrives. Jamaican stars of Boys Soccer peer from the hall into the briefly open door. They themselves have already removed shirts, and catcalls go both ways. Jamar, wearing his National Team headband, salutes Schuyler as she struts in.

"Hey dere, Schuyler. When ya gonna let me take you out, girl?" His accent is deep.

Schuyler nods at his body: "I heard I can't handle you, big fella."

Jamar blows a kiss. They've been flirting forever.

When Laine walks in Nikki waves shyly. Laine either doesn't see or doesn't want to respond.

Parker rolls her eyes. "Geez-*us*, I thought your crush was over. What's the deal?"

"It would just be nice to get along. We live together for God's sake," Nikki says grumpily, and they prepare to head out to the dining hall. *Why can't I give up?*

Varsity lockers aren't tin. The oak cupboards have brass placards engraved with the player's name. Laine gets butterflies opening hers: *Laine Hunt, Lower-form, Greenwich, CT.*

Laine's shin pads are streaked with mud, cleats clotted with grass. As she strips her dank clothes, Heather alights next to her.

"You were awesome today, Lainer. Seriously, we're better this year. We needed a strong center. You *do* realize that you might start, and MK might sit."

Laine smiles. "Thanks. Yeah, the MK thing is a little weird, right?"

"No way. She just has to deal with it." Heather leans against a locker to watch Nikki and Parker exit, and taps Laine's knee. "So what's up with your roommate?"

"What do you mean?"

Heather shrugs. "I don't know. I mean, what's her *issue?*"

Heather is the archetypal bridesmaid. She precedes Schuyler like secret service. Laughs raucously even before she's gotten Schuyler's jokes. *Somehow I can imagine Heather giving Schuyler a sponge bath, pressing the wet cloth to her forehead with all tenderness. Maybe sucking the water out after.* When these two walk across the quad, even though they're the same height, Schuyler's taller. If they have the same cash in hand, Schuyler's richer. The only thing Heather can do better than Schuyler is kiss Schuyler's ass and be her best friend.

Laine hangs her musty T-shirt on the hook. She's unwilling to take off her sports bra during this exchange so she folds her arms. "I mean, I'm not sure. She had a really different childhood and stuff."

"You know she's been hanging around Seth Walters? You know him?"

"I know who he is." *Am I on trial here?*

"Did you know he and Schuyler used to be together? He's a senior. I feel bad for Nikki, because Schuyler heard he and your roommate had sex in the auditorium Tuesday night. Ashley Browning saw them."

"I didn't know." *I don't* want *to know.*

"Is she on the pill?" Heather asks. "Her tits are *huge.*"

"There's my star center." Schuyler walks up, rubbing her hair with a towel. "So I heard your roommate had a wild one Tuesday night."

"I guess so. She didn't say anything."

"Well, all the Seniors know *Lolita* from Long Island now!" Schuyler laughs as if this is funny.

"Are you talking about Nikki the two-dollar trick?" Rory calls down the bench.

Heather guffaws, tossing her reddish hair back.

"Now, now," Schuyler says, smiling, putting one foot into her Cosabella thong. "We shouldn't be cruel." Meaning: *Isn't it so fun to be cruel?* "And just for the *record,* Seth was fine for the time, but she can have him. I've moved on, thank you very much, to bigger and richer, baby."

Schuyler is gorgeous in clothes, throws it around. But

sometimes, straight from the shower, hair slicked and sternum uncovered, her body is startling. Laine can see details of her skull, and the barbed components of her shoulder—like a cricket or a walking thinspo.

MK, on the other hand, lounges and goofs and struts. Her thighs in the back are dimpled, shoulders big, tits tiny, waist narrow. A gold chain with a tiny heart swings from her neck. She told Laine her dad had given it to her; that was in the beginning of the season. MK doesn't talk to Laine so much anymore, and in fact walks past them all now without glancing. Everyone's quiet as she passes in her vintage ski sweater and pom-pom hat, rubbing Carmex into her lips, as though they're trading state secrets.

"Hurry up and get showered, Laine," Schuyler barks. "Walk with us to Miss H's."

In a private moment Schuyler and Laine have exiting the room, Schuyler says quietly: "Honestly, aside from the bet and stuff, if Nikki ever cruises or has Seth ever or smokes or drinks, any of that, you gotta tell me. Not to snitch, but because it's better if I know. I'm her proctor. Her safety is my liability, and that girl, she's definitely unsafe."

"Right," Laine says. *How transparent can you be?* Laine feels smothered. *Why am I involved? I want nothing to do with this.*

And at the same time, she sometimes notes in herself a

small thrill of being included. Like now, as the group makes its way over dark lawn to the coach's place, Schuyler puts her arm around Laine's shoulders and goes on one of her unprovoked let-me-tell-you-how-it-is diatribes. "Honestly? You're going to love this place, Lainer. The people that are, you know, good, *the good ones*, are so fabulous, you will make the best friends of your life."

Miss Hartford's apartment in Appleby is like a dorm room grown up: walls painted Nantucket Red and hung with Taft and Dartmouth awards, dumbbells in the corner, tartan curtains. Seniors lounge on couches, Upper-forms and Lower-forms on the floor, as per tradition. Eating together here, Miss H explains now, is ritual too.

"We'll do this at least once a week, to remember we're family. Win or lose—*family*."

Laine hangs on every word. *This is why I'm here*, she thinks.

"One more practice before our first game. What's being passed around the room is the game-day lunch menu. Items *highlighted* are the ones you should eat. Now I want you players to go over some technique with me here."

They watch footage of last year's game against Taft, and rewind and review different plays. Miss H wants them to visualize plays while they fall asleep, while they wait in line at the dining hall. "Make a movie. Watch yourself play."

After an hour of watching and talking field hockey,

they're done. "Let's eat!" Miss H says.

As the girls giggle through *Entourage*, MK grabs a third slice of pizza. As she reaches she gets a shoulder squeeze.

Miss Hartford smiles and teases her: "MK, is that your *third*? You've got to run tomorrow, girl, we can't have a belly full of cheese."

"I'm starving!" MK says, blushing.

"Have an apple, silly," Miss H answers, tossing her a Granny Smith.

Laine couldn't even eat one slice. She can practically see food move through her body, as though she was made of transparent tubes. She knows the chemistry of food groups, and hates grease soiling her bloodstream. If she eats too much for the amount of exercise completed, her muscles start to turn from iron to Styrofoam in a matter of hours. Laine looks at MK now, at her big gold hoops and corduroy blazer. Sometimes, on the field, Laine smells the hippie perfume-oil called Rain that MK wears sweating off into the breeze. It almost repulses her, and she doesn't know why.

Overall, though, by the time the team is putting on J. Crew scarves and pulling hoods over their heads to meet an early, errantly cool night, Laine has forgotten everything except these people, this family, the warm room. The night reminds her of the Sundays her aunt and uncle and cousins came for spaghetti and a ping-pong tournament in the basement or backgammon tournament in the den. Thomas would play the Beatles' *White Album* over and over, and no one was happy when it was time to say good night. So the grown-ups let the kids stay up while they had one more glass of wine upstairs. The dog chased the Ping-Pong ball when it bounced on the floor, and Laine got a stomachache from cupcakes and still fell into heavenly little-kid sleep.

She can tell she's not the only one who feels at home tonight. Faces are bright and cheery as they thank Miss H and zipper their jackets.

What Seth and Nikki are doing, Nikki has no idea. She wouldn't call it going out or dating or being friends. Or being strangers. She doesn't know what they are. He never IMs or calls. So it's a matter of seeing him around, and waiting for him, and thinking about him, and then being with him when chance arranges it. And Nikki has no one to analyze and strategize with—conversations about sex and love were primary in friendships at home. Only a couple times has Parker shyly asked a question. But he's become her armor; belonging to him makes her feel better about not quite belonging, yet, to Wellington.

The window between the end of study hall and curfew, 9:30 to 10 at night, is Break, and has more power than any half hour should. Lower-forms establish themselves and Upper-forms preen at the clubhouse, while couples quickly do what they do—in secret but public places on the 1,165-acre grounds. It is *the* social time. During the rest of the day, kids are in class, or desperately napping, studying, playing sports, or calling home. After the first month a society forms among new students, and the old hierarchy absorbs it—the social topography at Break is rough terrain, navigable only by the dexterous. Freaks and geeks feel a cold wind when they enter the room.

This is when Nikki often meets Seth. They walk to some lonely place—the radio station room, to which Seth has a key, or if it's not freezing, the lake where the night woods are reflected upside down—and hang out. Hookup spots are well catalogued, and reserved by way of seniority. The limited options means that sometimes Preps and Lower-forms crowd into one space, and have to overhear one another's sweet-nothings and unzippering. Innovation is key: The phone booth doors have windows at the top, but a guy can pretend to talk while he gets a blow job down below. There are couches that will get a girl pregnant if she sits down on them—like the purple velvet cushions on the choir loft pews, pillows practically crystallized with organic matter.

Sometimes he's so glad to see her he picks her up when he hugs her. But never in front of anyone. In fact, near large groups, he backs away preemptively. He never asks where she's going to be, or when. *It's funny, because at home a guy practically latches his girl's ankle with a probation bracelet.*

A Long Island guy holds his girl in public, usually with her standing in front of him and his hands clasped around her midriff, touching her ass, kissing her neck—marking her like a jaguar rubs musk on everything to claim it. *Not Seth.*

She saw him a couple days ago, shirt untucked and hanging below the hem of his jacket, books on the crook of his forearm, walking down Cranberry Hall.

"Don't got the time, babe, even if I do got the inclination," he said then, raising his hand to high five, then taking it away at the last moment to mess with her.

She knows that stuff like that is usually a performance for Diego, or whoever he's with, but occasionally it seems like a sourness, a bitterness at life, that catches up to him, that once in a while takes him down.

Often they just play. When he doesn't shower, he smells of nicotine and sandalwood and greasy hair. She pretend-hits him, tells him to bathe or he ain't getting nothing. *I thought you liked me dirty,* he says. *Not this kind of dirty,* she says, *you're just nasty.*

But tonight, in the closed-up auditorium, they sit in seats, pressed together like illicit lovers at some old movie theater. They don't talk. She rakes his corduroy thigh, as if doing it mindlessly, casually. She kisses him, barely, wetly, biting his bottom lip as she retreats. Runs her nails down his neck. He almost looks sad, his head tilted down, but it's the way a guy looks when things are getting urgent, when he's waiting, when he's trying to contain his instincts. She leans to whisper, pressing against him, then leans back, taking it away, then brushes him when leaning forward again, then she laughs in the big quiet dark. She puts her hands there, she feels what's there, hot under denim. *Nicole,* he groans finally, and takes her face in his hands.

Laine knocks on Schuyler's door to get the grapes she left in her fridge.

"Lainer, I ate some, totally hope you don't mind," Schuyler says, handing over a mostly bare stem and grabbing a couple more grapes. "I'll get you back."

As Laine leaves, Schuyler points to the book. "I got some nice material here, wanna see?"

Um, no. "Sure."

Schuyler has printed Nikki's MySpace blog and tucked it into the bet book. As Laine looks, she also sees written on Nikki's page: "50% Italian, 50% Jewish." She looks at Schuyler inquisitively.

"Yeah, I got her *stats,* you know? Her mom's Jewish. Doesn't that make so much sense? I was like, *Right, I get it.*"

"How did you, I mean . . ."

"I just freakin' asked her! I was like, *Aren't you part Jewish?*"

Laine thinks it's weird to say the word aloud. She's used

to people leaving it out. As in: *He's so generous,* with the "for a Jew" left off the end. *She's incredibly understated.* Laine doesn't believe she herself has prejudices, but that's because they're unsaid. Laine inherited notions she's never examined, like a safe-deposit box of heirlooms she'll never use or wear but will simply hand down in a will to the next generation.

When Laine opens her own door, Nikki's in bed, gilded by apricot light. Her cheeks pink, hair tangled, legs sprawling out of a mint-green negligee. Like a kid. No foul language, no swagger, nothing to prove.

But Nikki's desk is a hill of coffee cups with lipstick stains, M&Ms bags, cell phone beeping as its battery dies, violet bra, a Sigur Ros CD burned by Seth, nail files, tissues, spilled glitter. On the floor, a froth of socks and panties and shoes. Laine turns off the lamp.

Lies in bed with eyes closed and can't let go. For some reason, she feels especially anxious. Even asleep, Nikki makes Laine see red. *Who raised this girl to think chewing gum loudly is cute, and boys and lip gloss and long, purposeless stories about friends back home are interesting, and roommates are supposed to be sisters?* The other day, things had gotten tense when Nikki had unwrapped a tampon and asked Laine to look the other way. Laine had to speak up: "Honestly, please don't do that in here."

Why can't she make it easier for other people to like her?

It would be easier on all of us. I'm living with the enemy.

Laine learned the cardinal rule at nine or ten. It was a spring afternoon, and she and a bunch of friends were playing badminton in the yard. The day was unnaturally hot, and Laine wore her bathing suit. Polly beckoned her to the porch. "Put clothes on, Laine. Everyone shouldn't have to look at you." *Everyone shouldn't have to look at you.*

But as the night seeps blackly into Laine now, darkening each cell of her mind, she thinks less and less straight. Her anger gets skewed, curves back to her. Fear makes chilled sweat. Laine tries to avoid thinking about anything, and when she does that, things creep into her. Tonight it's her old house, the quince branches growing into her mouth, their ebony branches sending out dusty-rose blossoms, cupboards in her conscience opening onto musty shelves of *National Geographic*s, the basement stairs yawning open inside her, her dad's shotguns shining dully, her mom's gum boots and garden tools glinting in her chest . . .

Light rain falls as Varsity makes their way down the hill to practice today, turning fields to slush. They play anyway.

They're doing 5 V 5 drills when it starts to pour. And it's a primitive joy that makes even the most stoic girls laugh. Lightning cracks on the field, and MK lifts her stick and tilts her face to the roaring sky and calls out—*"Strike me!"* She even drops to her knees in the mud, which doesn't matter because the girls are covered from head to toe. Laine gets caught in a whirl of girls holding one anothers' arms and swinging the line around in a wild circle. Blind with rain.

Lightning again, breaking the gray clouds with fire.

"Okay, we've met our match," Miss H yells over the storm. "We get the picture. Let's wrap it up, players."

The team is reluctant to end early, which has never happened. In the showers they're giddy and loud, trying to scorch the cold damp out of their bones. Rory figures out how to blow bubbles from a shampoo bottle. Laine closes her eyes, runs scalding water over her face and down her silky white hair and down her back, and she smiles. Caught in the inside of something for once. MK sings a rendition of "Here Comes the Rain Again," and even catches Laine's eye, smiles,and winks.

Walking back, jackets pulled over their heads, the group's energy stays high in the rain. Laine sneaks looks at MK, flooded with relief at being forgiven, or whatever it is that's happening here. Laine knows she's a threat to MK's position. She hates it, almost as much as she loves to win the game.

She's always been sensitive to rifts. Even as a child she sensed fractures and closed them. On the beach, her mom, in a white tunic and tortoiseshell glasses, sat under the umbrella, scowling for unknown reason, while Thomas played with the girls. So Laine made her mom help bury Laine in the sand, and Polly reluctantly found rocks for buttons. A summertime snowman. Thomas, Chris, and Maggie helped smooth Laine's new body over her true body, until Laine laughed and the thing cracked. Soon Thomas was holding green sea glass to Polly's ears as jewelry, Polly holding her own hair back and modeling with mock vanity.

Sometimes a bell chimes on Lancaster Four, ringing in some kind of jovial hour. It's happy-go-lucky time, everyone rambunctious and playful. Like siblings in a big house, although they act like something besides sisters, and yet they're not brothers either. A hybrid.

"Dude, who took my last beef jerky?"

"No one wants your jerky, you psycho," someone is replying even as someone else is slowly looking away, turning toward the wall as if examining something of stunning interest.

Dawn gets crucified for her hygiene cabinet: Metamucil, Vagisil, Monostat, Midol. "What else you got, dental dams?"

But her effortless, Midwestern way of laughing it off wins them over every time.

They play field hockey on the carpet with someone's stale Powerbar. A Kelly Clarkson CD is stomped with cleats. Girls suck Skoal Bandits and play Texas Hold 'Em, listen to Johnny Cash.

Aya and Parker have bonded. They drink white tea and eat Turkish rose candy and look at books on Cindy Sherman, Duchamp, Cassavetes. Online they visit websites of Thai graffiti artists and look at drawings of California inmates and listen to pirate radio from an expat community on the Ivory Coast. Aya makes statements like: "Think of Wellington as an aging man. Too insecure to let a girl be confident so he works to keep her down, but desires that girl beyond all else." And: "As Rilke said, girls, 'Live the questions,' that's our only option. Write it on your hand and don't forget it."

Sometimes Nikki's jealous of Aya and Parker, and sometimes she thinks they're isolated in their den of bohemia and avant-garde gadgets.

Gray afternoon. Not lonely so much as gentle, the sky supple like velour. Crows fight on the dying lawn. Nikki comes out of Psych 103 with a head of statistics and a notebook of assigned work. This is her favorite class even though it brings her down. They're reading studies of abused boys in the 1970s foster care system—she just watched a man's memories videotaped in his jail cell. She checks e-mails at the library, and finds dynamite in her in-box.

· · ·

Subject: the juice

Baby girl, baby girl, what is up??!!??? How come you never IM me no more? You don't bring me flowers . . . anymore. So how's Waddington or Wellingbutt or wherever you're at? Truss me life sux ballz here. By that I mean ain't nuthin changed darling. My dad's trying to force me to work weekends at ye olde Blockbuster. I'd rather cut myself. Let's see. Kim and Rod hooked up. She went from hating him to digging on him. Go figure. But then she did Jimmy Barroli the next weekend at Jones Beach bonfire. She handed it ALL OUT like candy and now it's GONE. She's a leper. Me and Stinger got down a little, no one knows, don't say anything. All I did was give him a hand with bizness (using some pomegranate ginger what-the-fuck body shop lotion he found in his sister's glove compartment!!!). I dunno. I been scheming and dreamin, baby girl, but it's not the same without you. Kick their asses up there in bumbletown usa. Proud of you nik. Big kiss from the island . . . xoxox ness

Out of the words blows a breeze of beer, Gucci Rush, the autumn beach at night, Vanessa's voice. She remembers briefly what it was like to be herself; it meant not having to use effort to remember what it was like to be herself. Now she keeps walking because it would be more painful to stop and feel what she's feeling.

But when she gets to the room, she sits on her bed and gazes at both closets. Laine's is a line of J.Crew and Ralph

Lauren clothes, shirts in colors like heather or oatmeal *or might as well be manure*, jodhpurs for fuck's sake, sweaters with moth holes that are in some way cool; *tell me how on earth an insect eating one's garment ends up being glamorous.*

And her own mess. Hangers twisted and crooked, the wood cubby jacked full of mesh and glitter and denim. At home, Nikki and her crew used to go into the city with someone's parents, allowed to hit 8th Street by themselves, walk-running in a gaggle from cheap store to trashy store, getting violet rip-off Chanel sunglasses here and white stretch jean shorts there and an acid green faux croc clutch at the stand on the sidewalk. Hitting S&M stores for sick bustiers and lace-up stilettos. Sephora for perfume, lip gloss in sugary watermelon, Stila blush.

Why don't I ask my dad to send me some orthopedic shoes and funeral clothes? Then I might fit in. She looks at her junk with disdain.

The game.

In the locker room, heads are down except for one—Laine stares at the coach. *I can fix this.* Laine spent the first half on the bench. Watching MK miss foul hits. Watching MK chop at sticks and get whistles.

"A bunch of wannabes are making you look like you don't even belong on the *Thirds* team. This is Millbrook for Christ's sake. They play the *handicap* schools and lose."

Miss Hartford's neck veins pulse. "If you all don't take your heads out of your kilts then it's going to be a really long season. Capeesh?"

Her tirades are legendary, but this one is early.

This game is just a warm-up before Founder's League season starts. Wellington reached finals last year, undefeated, before losing to Deerfield, but now a 2–1 halftime deficit has somehow caught the team off-guard. "All right, we're going to mix things up next half. Williams, you're in for Kiersten at right fullback. Hunt, you're in for MK on the second midfield line. Okay. We all know we are *superior*. Now play like it. Huddle up. 1, 2, 3, Lions!!"

It's on, Laine thinks, but as she makes her way back down to the field past the SUVs and luxury sedans grafittied with prep school and Ivy League bumper stickers and preppy vanity plates, she glances sideways at MK.

Somehow, for Laine, MK getting demoted is connected to her decadences, to that third slice of pizza, to caring too much about blue jeans and boys, to being too pretty, to being careless. Laine feels guilty about her part, yet believes this replacement is inevitable.

Before the whistle, Miss Hartford pulls Laine aside. "Laine, get into the moment, now. Remember your sprint mechanics."

A dead-on pass, a downfield streak, a dodge, a shot, and the game's tied. Laine is right: She can fix it. In fact, all of a sudden, she's fixed much more. The awkward introductions, gossip, lame orientation events, and preseason jitters is erased. Here come the high fives, the thumbs-ups, the applause. MK fusses with her mouthguard, looking anywhere but at the celebration.

Here comes the rain again.

8

The middle of October brings a truly cool spell, finally, that breaks coats out of dry-cleaner wrapping and mittens out of drawers. English 204 is a sociable group, even if it is at eight A.M. Sociable except for Laine, who sits across from her roommate but can't meet her eyes. Instead, she looks out the window at fallen leaves whipped in tornado circles.

"All right, what do we think?" James Ballast asks his bleary-eyed students. He loves the challenge. No one stirs. No hands rise. "Come on, guys, we got heterosexuality, bisexuality, asexuality, homosexuality, designer labels, movie stars, and enough drugs to get you all wired. Dobbs, what are you thinking? Why are we reading this?"

Chase can barely keep his eyes open at this hour. His

hair hasn't been cut since he arrived so it's jagged. He's abandoned coat and tie and embraced coat and turtleneck, an approved variation of the dress code. He stares at the wall—maybe if he looks long enough somehow Mr. Ballast will forget he called on him or someone else will chime in.

Ballast can't help but smile as Chase chews the end of his turtleneck. As it inches up closer to his nose he looks like a prep school extremist—nothing but eyes. "Dobbs. I'm coming back to you. Wake up, let's get rolling here."

The kids love Ballast. He never bores them. But as the years pass, and the world scares him more and more, he's started to teach with a sort of eloquent desperation. His dream is to fire them up, and he shows them tapes of the Watts riots, marches on Washington, Civil Rights gatherings. He knows that later on these kids may have the power to do great things, but he fears they want to run the world rather than live in it and love it and change it.

Nikki sits next to Chase, and can tell he likes this material but holds back with Noah there to lampoon every comment. Nikki spent her Sunday afternoon tearing through *Less Than Zero*, even though the class was only required to read one-fourth of the book.

"I mean, Mr. B," she speaks up. "I think we all know people like this, which is why it's so great. I mean, I even feel like I could live in that world. And besides, who's to say that Chase and Noah don't hook up with each other

116

every night, right?"

The class laughs.

Laine shudders in her seat. *God, why does she always make such a scene?* Nikki catches her eye and Laine looks away. Nikki rolls her eyes.

Mr. Ballast takes an admonitory tone as he sits on the table. "Look, guys. We can talk about this stuff but you must act mature." He looks for a moment at the class, whispers: "I mean, this is *intense* stuff, right?"

Greg jumps in. "A'ight. I mean you got this dude, Clay, right? Is he strung out though? Because the dude's hitting lines all day, but then he has these flashbacks. You know? So can you trust what he's saying? He keeps wanting to go back to when it was simpler, so why don't he just get it *together*. I have a hard time feeling sympathy."

"He doesn't want sympathy. This is his life." Nikki gets animated, one arm akimbo, the other gesturing. "He wants to, like, get high and vanish. I know people like this."

"You're from the Island, doll. The only thing your crew gets high off is hair product," Noah says under his breath.

Laine squirms. She hates English 204. She never has anything to add, even when she's painstakingly read the book.

"Nihilism," Ballast says, after everyone stops laughing. "That's what Clay *seems* to be exercising. He wants to be free, he wants to be invincible, and so this is the route he's trying. He's looking for something by way of nothing."

"Good luck," Jasper whispers.

"Where did Gatsby look for it?" Ballast asks.

After a moment, he calls on Gabriel. Gabriel looks unsure. Ballast prompts him, "Did Gatsby break rules like this? Was his treasure outside the society?"

"He looks for it in society. In *following* rules, I guess."

Chase always twirls his hair when he says something in earnest, like he does now. "Mr. B, the only thing, thus far, keeping Clay from living a normal life is his family, right? And his family is his society, really. And his society is toxic. The anorexic sisters looking for blow, divorced parents in Hollywood. It's not a sex thing, it's not a drug thing—the kid just has no base. His vacations are all fu . . . sorry." Ballast nods his head for Chase to continue. "His vacation homes are supposed to be sanctuaries, but he just gets messed up to avoid facing himself. I mean, shit, look at all the kids here who do it."

"This is all good stuff, guys!" Ballast slaps Chase five as he races by to the eraser board, messes up Nikki's hair, gives Jasper a little knock to the head.

Laine doesn't know she's staring at Chase when she is. Her boy fantasies are tourettic and primordial, and unwelcome. Whenever she catches herself at it, she turns scarlet. Her imaginings take place in an unknown place, at an unknown time. Ardor without a body. She thinks of Chase in shadow, tries to see how he would see her—her face gazing, troubled, out the window—and he will wonder what bothers her. *Or he'll see me scorch down the field, thighs pumping under my kilt.* Somehow he'll manage to find her in a heartbreaking posture, and want to marry her—

"Come on, my little Kerouacs, let's go the distance! Where do you find freedom? In abiding by laws and beating everyone at their own game?" As he talks he maniacally scribbles quotes with marker. "Or in breaking them? Here, Peter Gabriel: 'I walked right out of the machinery/My heart going Boom Boom Boom.' Now who doesn't get goosebumps hearing that? I mean, that's exciting. Who decides for you how to live?"

"The trustees of Wellington," Noah mutters.

Chase and I would get married in Charleston, I'd wear Elsa's ivory dress and carry magnolias—

"It would seem so. But *you* do. Of course, it's you. You want in, or you want out? And here," Ballast says, ink staining his fingers as he writes. "Mary Oliver. Anyone? Poet, natural world. Laine, read this for everyone."

Laine sits up, clears her throat. "Uh, 'Tell me, what else should I have'—what is that?" Laine is unprepared. She mumbles. She looks around the class and sees Nikki staring at her. She pauses, losing her place.

Nikki senses her discomfort. *I don't think Laine has looked at me all day.*

"'Should I have done,'" says Ballast.

"'Doesn't everything die,' *wait*, 'doesn't everything die—'"

"You're doing fine, Laine," Ballast says.

"'—at last, and too soon? Tell me, what is it you plan to do with your one wild and precious life?'"

The bell rings and everyone starts to pack up. Ballast speaks over the noise: "I ask you to think about this: We're reading a book that some claim celebrates death of spirit. Yet the book itself is a work of art, it was *created* by someone, it was made out of nothing. That's what creation is." He raises his voice to compete with the chaos. "And Bret Easton Ellis wrote this when he was just a few years older than some of you. Do me a big old favor and think on that, my friends."

Nikki does a mime's wave at Laine. "Hello?"

Laine is on fire from stuttering. She waves back, barely. "I see you, what?"

"Jesus, nothing I guess."

Nikki stands back to let Laine pass.

It's beautiful out, and Laine has three periods free. She thinks about napping in the room but Nikki's headed toward the dorm. She wanders to the snack bar but sees Schuyler and Heather with Senior guys and just can't handle it. Schuyler and Heather have become rabid over the *stupid bet, that screwed-up game.* Last night they'd coaxed her into Heather's room, where they were binging on raw cookie dough and gazing at the bet book. The five contenders' pages were covered in memorabilia and quotes. The book was addictive: the girls looked with wet eyes. It was pornography of superiority.

Schuyler had licked her fingers and stabbed the cover. "Laine, this is priceless, this is the kind of, like, legendary tradition that people write about when they write about boarding schools. You feel me? It's totally crazy."

Laine stands on the lawn now, her blood doing a low-grade sizzle. She finds herself on Laurel Trail, which leads away from fields, from class buildings, from dorms. To the stable.

She approaches cautiously, but no one's there. She's about to enter the barn, and suddenly a guy appears. "Do you need something?" Trevor is standing on the side of the structure, hosing off his boots, wearing an Audioslave T-shirt, and his truck is an old Chevy, pale cream with banana stripes. A patchouli air freshener hangs with rosary beads from the giant rearview mirror, and a small animal skull is bleaching on the dash. At the last moment, a mutt puts her head up from sleeping on the front seat.

"Are you a rider?" he asks, coiling the hose on its wheel.

"Well, not here."

He smiles. "That's not what I asked."

"I'm a rider."

"Chaplin needs a ride. The girl supposed to work him never showed today. Feel up to it?"

Laine smiles. *Hell yes.*

Chaplin is a big guy, and he carries her slowly up the path to the woods. Drags his heavy hooves through late-blooming white roses that are tangled up in the red leaves—leaves that are glassine, the daylight coming through them. Chaplin's horseshoes thud the earthen path. Apples fallen from arthritic trees rot in tall grass, giving off a vinegar-vanilla smell. They enter deeper, truer, bluer woods. She indulges in rich oxygen as they pass through the calm. They reach an opening, an ochre meadow with a sinuous trail. She spurs Chaplin to a gallop, but she can feel within a few paces it's not what he wants.

So they slow.

They slow some more.

She drapes herself forward, holds his neck, puts her face to his hot, bristly hide. Their hearts beat in opposite rhythms. She feels the fullness that comes before crying, that dark red swelling in her throat or breast, but she's not sad, and the feeling doesn't become tears.

Instead, strangely enough, she almost falls asleep. She lies there, eyes closed, and lets Chaplin walk. She listens to his blood move, the way you can hear your own underwater. And then she smells the apples.

Chaplin has brought her back to the stable. She looks

up, groggy, into Trevor's eyes.

"Take a little nap there?" he asks, trying to betray no judgment.

Laine shakes her head to clear it. "I don't know." She gives a husky laugh as she slides down. She brushes her jeans, looks at Trevor again. "He's a good horse."

Trevor seems to decide on forgiving Laine for being weird. "Yeah," he says easily now, "he's one righteous horse. Me and him agree on all important things. You know?"

Laine laughs again. She unbuckles Chaplin's bridle, rubs his jaw for him in a way she knows will ease soreness.

"You new here?"

"Yup."

"You're not by any chance in Apple-something dorm, with Jenny Briggs? She's the one who never showed."

"No, Lancaster."

"How you like this place?"

Laine shrugs.

"I'm Trevor, by the way."

"Laine," she says, and knows she should move forward and shake hands but is nervously rooted to the ground, which often happens. "You go to the local school?" she asks him.

"Glendon Public."

"You work here every day?"

His beeper goes off. "I got to go pick up my girlfriend. Uh, no, more like every other. I do firewood with my uncle otherwise. No offense, but I couldn't handle being here every day. You got some *pricks* up in there."

Laine looks at him—he scrubs his hands in an ancient white sink with periwinkle stains, shakes his hands dry, rubs them on his jeans.

"I don't know why you would expect me not to be offended," she says.

He looks now at her with alarm, starts to apologize.

"But I'm not," she continues.

He laughs. Laine is peeking into the stalls as she prepares to leave. A roan mare with a huge belly looks to Laine, and Laine rubs her chin.

"How far?" Laine asks.

"She's gonna foal in about a week and a half or so. Depends on the moon."

"Take care," Laine says, turning in the golden-lit grass and starting back up the path.

Trevor pauses as he gets into his squeaky-door truck. "Come on down here anytime. You can always ride. Hey, I'll come get you if she starts to labor."

"That would be great," Laine says, smiling, knowing he'll do no such thing but appreciating the gesture.

Plan B for Nikki and Parker has turned out to be Woods

Crew. Also called Would Screw.

They weaseled out of Thirds and into this special project, an escape hatch for nonathletes, stoners, and eco-freaks. Four days a week, they pile into a monster Suburban with glassless windows and no seats, and truck deep into the forest to chop wood, rebuild cabins, or make other adjustments to the land.

Most of their tools are ancient, even esoteric, oiled by years of palms and use, but they also use new stuff. It took two weeks for the transfer, and today's their first day. They're reshingling Maggie's Farm, a cabin in the east section of the woodlands.

Mr. Grant is the overseer, but everyone just calls him Grant. He's from New Zealand—black hair tied behind his head and a face so angular he's genuinely ugly. He sucks licorice shipped from his hometown, and anyone who's ever tried one promptly spit it out. He teaches philosophy and astronomy.

He picks them up outside Blackstick, and Nikki crouches in the truck bed so as not to dirty her white Baby Phat sweatpants.

"You must be joking," Linden Braddle says, an Oregon-born progressive Upper-form who demonstrates by his loose, familiar posture how close he and nature are. "You're going to be covered in soil and debris at the end of this, so you might as well give in now."

Everyone in the rocking truck snickers, but Nikki squats on. "Yo, I'm not ten years old, I'm not going to roll around in dead leaves and shit." But she likes that everyone is watching her.

At the site, Grant passes out nail aprons, hammers, ladders. They discuss basics: never put nails between your teeth, never drop a hammer to the ground, never let go of a ladder someone is climbing even if it seems steady. The air is a bit cool in the woods, and steam comes from Grant's mouth. Nikki looks to Parker, who seems thrilled to be out here, and asks if this is maybe worse than Thirds.

"You're gonna get into it," Parker says. "Just wait."

"Hi, my name is Nikki, have we met?" Nikki stands there in the clearing, waving around her hammer. "Look at me. I'm wearing an effing *nail apron*. What *is* this?"

"You put your nails in the pockets."

"Parker, I know. My point is that I belong in a cozy Starbucks right now, listening to my iPod and drinking hot chocolate, and instead I'm standing next to you in the jungle, waiting to build a house or some shit. It's cold, and there's *dirt* everywhere."

"It's called *earth*, in this context," Linden chimes in.

"Linden, you're painful. Why don't you go round up some *foliage* and shove it up your ass?"

Parker laughs as Linden ambles away defeated, congratulates Nikki: "Way to play nice, babe."

Nikki spends the afternoon hovering uncertainly on the periphery of any real work being done. Kids strip old shingle off the roof, calling as they drop pieces, "Coming down." Nikki keeps dodging falling tar paper.

"Okay, you know what? I'm just going to get out of the way."

In the truck on the way back, Grant calls back to Nikki in his accent: "Nicole, you have great spirit. But you are wildly unhelpful."

"What! I picked up tar paper and put it in the bin!"

"Tomorrow I want to see you up on the ladder."

"Holy shit," Nikki, still squatting, mutters to Parker. "I feel like I'm on a chain gang or something."

The next day Parker dresses Nikki up in old Levis and a flannel shirt. Nikki squeals, looking in the mirror: "I look like Paul Bunyan's love kid. This is awesome!"

It's a gray day, with a lick of bitterness, but the woods are still. Nikki and Parker stand on ladders and take a lesson from Grant on using a level. He points out the liquid in the glass bubble in the center of the tool. "Use this to mark your lines. Take your pencil, and mark like this . . ." He demonstrates. "Then take your chalk string, like this—and draw your line. That's how we'll align the new shingles."

Parker and Nikki work at this all afternoon, talking to the other kids on ladders or on the ground, listening to the background music of nails banged into wood. Caroline Camper is a brawny redhead who comes off angry at first, but is actually feisty. She tells compulsive stories like an overexcited ten-year-old boy, but they usually have people laughing. Nikki goes from not liking her to revering her a bit.

Nikki even gets used to her pockets of tools, and makes straight lines with growing expertise. When she and Parker remove the last shingles at the peak of the roof, they discover names and dates in pencil. It looks like it was written today, but the date is 1932.

"Grant!" Parker yells. "Look at this!"

Everyone crowds around. Nikki asks why it looks so new. Grant tells them it's because those guys shingled the roof right. Then he tells them all to add their names.

"You guys are shingling well. No rain, no snow will touch your signatures. Don't forget to put the date, so kids down the line will know when you were here."

After Parker and Nik sign the wood, they look at each other. And smile.

No Woods Crew on Wednesday, and Nikki feels lost. On Thursday she's waiting at Blackstick, leaning against the building in the sun, before the truck even pulls up. The group divides, and Grant hauls logs with Parker and Nikki into the firewood-chopping clearing. Nikki asks if Linden doesn't drive him crazy.

"Nikki!" Parker chides her.

"Well, I'm curious, because it's so obvious Linden goes

around *copying* Grant," Nikki says.

Grant slaps his gloves together and bits of bark and dust fly. "I don't mind the question. And I don't mind Linden. I enjoy him, actually."

"But, like, he goes around checking on us all to see if we're doing work right, and then, like, gives us nature lessons about what bird we hear and stuff. Like, what's up?"

Grant rubs his hollow cheek, leaves a smudge. He smiles. "He's trying to become someone. He's on his way. People at your age make the same mistake, which you're making now. You get caught up in not looking stupid, but that means you hang back, yeah? And miss out on the messy process of becoming someone. Of living."

"I think I am becoming someone, though, aren't I?" Parker asks.

Grant picks up his ax, and taps a wedge into the log's end, and laughs. "You probably are, Parker. God, you should have seen me at fifteen. What a disaster," he twangs. "First I did nothing but obsess about my hair and my jeans. Then I went full force into the life of the mind, and didn't bathe. Protesting this, and speaking out against that. I was wrong about most of those issues, maybe eighty percent of the time. But I'm glad I went for it."

He slams the wedge and the log splits. "Not like I know I'm right and perfect now, yeah? Still fluid."

They chop wood for a half hour, then regroup. They're

all supposed to start work clearing a path, but it's transformed into such a gloriously sunny day that Grant tells them to take a hike or a nap in the sun, and then to come back to the truck at parting time.

"Just enjoy yourself," he says. "This is a golden day."

So Nik and Parker let Linden take them to Sleepy Rock, a jutting, smoothed boulder in the lake. They have to work their way through dense underbrush because the established trail doesn't lead here. Linden is proud of his find, which he came across one day exploring. He alternately hurries and then waits.

"Oh my God," Parker says. "This is heaven."

They're all lying on their backs on the stone, which is already warm. The air is cool but the sun toasts their bodies. The lake sucks at the rock. Their eyes are closed, legs crossed at ankles, arms crossed behind heads as pillows.

9

Laine gets up, groggy, at some hour close to dawn. Walks, bleary, to the bathroom, fluorescent hall lights blinding. Even at this hour, it comes down the hall like malodorous breath. She hears the night whisper it with halitosis: *bet bet bet bet bet . . .*

Earlier she'd seen the five girls in Schuyler's room, and the snickering and whispering made it obvious they were going through the book. *God, it's strange, this duel they've arranged, these gladiators they've dumped into this amphitheater. Girls fighting unknown demons in the dust, unaware that anyone's watching. They're struggling to last. They know they're bleeding but they keep on.*

Snack bar, Friday night. Nikki stands in line behind Jorgen, who hasn't shaken the nickname Napoleon D after the dance episode, as the bar fills. Jorgen is carrying music sheets; he's coming from the private practice room that he gets for study hall since he's a prodigy. He has a habit of waiting till he's at the front of the line before deciding what to order. And every day, like clockwork, he orders chicken nuggets, thus infuriating Nikki.

"What es 'Wank' Burger again?" Jorgen appears genuinely intrigued by the menu: Wank Burger, Jamison Nubs, 10:01s. Jamison Nubs are chicken nuggets named after a professor, Armand Jamison, who lost four fingers in a fishing accident. 10:01 is a peanut butter milk shake, and a Wellington remedy for party kids as it disguises alcohol on the breath.

Nikki cuts in. "Jesus, Jorgen. It's a goddamn cheeseburger with *mayo*. You get the same thing every night and it's not a Wank Burger. Order it and hurry up."

Trips laughs at their pseudo-fight. He's already thrown nuggets in the fryer for Jorgen. The kids love Trips because he sells pot and regales everyone with tall tales of the seventies starring guitar-playing trollops and medicine men and unicorns. He's one of many who wandered here from the city and never left. And he can see that Jorgen does this to make Nikki crazy, and that Nikki loves the ritual.

Chase, Noah, Greg, and Gabriel are sitting in a corner booth, leafing through a Facebook. Laine is in the other corner with field hockey girls, and Nikki makes sure not to even glance in her direction before sitting with the boys.

Laine watches out of the corner of her eye. *Look at that, and she's going to sit right next to Chase, too. That girl is out of control.* In fact, Rory is interrogating Laine now, offering a Butterfingers milk shake for info on Nikki's sexcapades. Rory mutters: "Find the blue dress, Lainer, and we'll get your girl impeached." As usual, under the inquisition of Schuyler and Company, Laine tries to laugh it off, to feed them little pieces that will keep them satisfied.

At the table Greg notices Nikki first, but with a certain kind of bravado makes no attempt to create space.

"Ew, loser. Let me sit." Nikki gives Greg a nudge with her hip.

"A'ight, but don't interrupt. We doin' a little recon work here, girl." Greg's braids are combed out and his Afro is high. In the month they've been at school, Greg has proved master of hairstyles. He's best friends with the old Russian guy who owns the barbershop in town.

"Are you all still rating people in that thing? I want to see me." Nikki grabs for the book, but is blocked calmly by Gabriel—no words, just calm action. These guys have bonded from living on the same floor, Nikki can tell.

Chase glances at her, but he's hard at work surveying the crowd. "Nice. All right, Gabe, check off that redhead Upper-Form. She's got a nice little backyard, too." Gabriel flips the pages and checks off another face.

Chase then addresses Nikki. "For your information, we *have* finished grading the Facebook. This is the opportunity book." Chase leans back in the booth like a small-town lawyer. "If you're out every night at this time, it means there's a chance. If we never see you, I seriously doubt any of us could bed you. See the logic?"

Nikki shakes her head, smiling. *He's not wrong.*

Chase continues, "Take you for instance, Nik. You're here every night–by our scientific analysis, what does that tell you?" Chase nudges Greg and the group cracks up.

"Okay, that's great, but what does it say that you guys are here more than me and none of you got a thing yet?"

"You need a formal invite or something?" Noah grinds his pelvis, and Nikki punches him in the arm.

"We've had this discussion–I don't do any dirty work unless I know you can return the favor with finesse, and none of you are qualified."

Noah shakes his head, grinning. "Ungrateful little tease."

This is where Nikki likes it, at the cozy center of a crew of boys, playing, bantering, nipping but not biting. Feeling fierce in her denim skirt, thigh-high suede boots, and Billabong hoodie. She's aware of older kids listening, girls rolling their eyes and guys smirking, but she's pretty sure they're also impressed at how she holds her own.

"Hey, C. I got another one. Asian girl coming out of the student center. She's semi-opportunity. I see her here every so often, don't you?" Noah nods at Mina, who's wearing a red mohair sweater and carrying a stack of library books.

The rest peer over to judge.

Chase looks down as though unimpressed. "She's in my math class, so what? I cheated off her last week and we both failed. Next."

But Greg has crossed his arms and is squinting at Chase. "Hmmmm."

Chase acts impatient with him. "What?"

"You got a crush on the Asian girl, that's what."

"Easy, Match-dot-com. Good call, except I don't." But Chase has a flush across his cheeks.

"Yeah, he doesn't care about Mina as much as he does about the snow princess over yonder," Noah says, jutting his chin at Laine.

The look that Chase gives Noah takes everyone by surprise. Even Noah backtracks. "Just kidding, totally kidding."

Chase won't look at Nikki.

It's 9:55, and the crowd begins filing back to their dorms. Greg is coaxing Mina over to Chase, who's putting up a fight, and Nikki is sad Seth never showed, and Gabriel is ordering microwaved chocolate-chip cookies to go, and they all get washed away in the tide of curfew.

Yellow leaves on the path are bright under a three-quarter moon, and everyone seems fired up by the same bedtime energy. Two guys duel with twigs. Girls walk back to Appleby with arms looped around one anothers' waists.

Nikki and Laine, for separate reasons, are exhausted, but Schuyler stands at the door. Laine peers at her alarm clock. 12:37 A.M.

"Evening, girls," Schuyler singsongs into their room.

"Schuyler?" Laine asks. "It's twelve thirty."

"I'm sorry, darlings, but tonight we're having a little hall party. Sort of an introduction, if you will, to becoming a Wellington woman." Schuyler pulls the elastic off her wrist and calmly puts up her hair. "Its fun. You'll learn so much about yourself." She starts to close the door and quietly adds, "By the way, wear underwear or a bathing suit, 'kay?"

Dawn, Charlotte, and Parker stand against Heather's bedroom wall. Dawn wears Panterra boxers and a purple sports bra that matches streaks she added to her hair. A metal choker gleams on her neck. Laine and Nikki join the lineup.

Schuyler marches, looks girls up and down. Rory and Heather laugh at nothing, out of the excitement of being in control.

"Hi, girls. You all look precious." Schuyler has a sly shimmer in her eyes. "Here's the thing. Every year we communicate to the younger girls that there is a hierarchy on this campus. This is a service, so you aren't kept in the dark. The reason we have you dressed in your underwear is so we can help you *improve*. No Wellington guy wants a girl with tubby legs, a fat stomach, or unsightly moles, right?"

The girls look down, confused, except for Nikki, who sneers at the Seniors—all of them on Zone bars, colonics, lemon juice, collagen, and cocaine. *Yeah, as if guys like girls with the taste of vomit lingering on their breath.*

"Are we ready?" Schuyler motions for the Senior girls to open their pens.

Nikki freezes. Laine and Parker each look down at the floor, their faces flushed red. Charlotte tries to disappear into the wall. Dawn laughs, takes a deep breath, arches her back, and extends her belly, "Start right here, get it over with."

Heather begins to work on Dawn.

On her belly: PREGNANT?

Her legs: LINEBACKER.

Over her chest: SAGGY TITS. And it's over for Dawn.

Laine is done by Schuyler, and gets off easy.

Her thighs: ATHLETIC.

Her stomach: ABS?

On her chest a simple remark, SOON, with a smiley face.

Why not write "Schuyler's Pet" across my heart?

Charlotte only gets one marking, but it's hard-core:

Schuyler writes the number of her plastic surgeon in Los Angeles on her cheek, with an arrow to her harelip.

Parker is trying to keep from shaking while Heather scribbles on her back. "Parker, stop moving."

Down her pale back: NICE FUCKING TAN.

Her ass: M.I.A.

A mole on the nape of her neck marked with a simple X.

Her toes spell out: DIRTY.

As Heather starts to write GREASY across her forehead, Nikki steps up to Parker and puts an arm over her. "Okay, she's done, Heather." Then she stares at Heather while speaking to Parker. "Don't worry, Heather's just mad cuz she has cankles. No amount of Trimspa or yacking can get rid of those logs."

Schuyler smiles slowly. "Your turn."

In two minutes, Nikki is a mural of expletives and circles.

Across the tip of her nose: SLUT.

Her forehead: MAFIA. Her chin: TRASH.

Arrows point to her groin on both legs. Across her left: CUM. Her right: DUMPSTER. Schuyler draws a penis going into her mouth with the initials L.I.E. (for the expressway) underneath.

Across her butt: NO LUBE NEEDED.

Her breasts: P.R. NIPS, standing for Puerto Rican nipples.

Dawn looks around. "This is so retarded I can hardly believe it."

Schuyler actually turns pink, knocked off course a degree by Dawn's casual condemnation. "Look guys, it was done to us. We had to pass along the tradition. It's what binds us all to each other, to this place. I mean, now this stuff is in the open, think of it that way! You guys did *great*, give yourselves a hand."

Laine watches Charlotte step back out of Schuyler's way as she walks like a soldier down the hall, tossing and catching her pen, whistling Christina Aguilera's "Beautiful."

Back in the room, Nikki and Laine walk around each other, like animals squaring off. Nikki finally asks how they could do this.

"Who's 'they'?" Laine asks. "You've pissed almost everyone off. You know who Seth is? He's your proctor's ex. You know what people saw you doing the other week? Think back and you'll probably figure it out."

"What are you talking about?"

"You're sleeping with someone you've known for like a month."

"Jesus Christ, are you saying what I think you're saying? Because—"

"No," Laine says flatly. "I'm not agreeing. I'm just saying you're making a really bad impression."

"*Fuck* you."

It hangs in the air.

"You know what, I'm not continuing this conversation,"

Laine says after a long silence, grabbing her towel and slamming the door.

Nikki puts on her black hoodie and jeans in the dark. She *wants* to disturb Laine's sleep. It's just after three.

Nikki cracks the door—first slowly, to let in light, but the door won't stop creaking so she jumps into the hallway. Heart thudding. Hands wet. No one in the hall. *Only four doors to get by and I got the stairwell,* she thinks. Nikki is a stone. *Please God let Schuyler sleep. Please God let Schuyler sleep.* Nikki speed-walks toward the hall's end, and sees the open bathroom door too late. *Oh, shit.*

Dawn peers out, saline solution in hand. She squints. "Subtle," she says. "One word of advice?"

Nikki's frozen.

"Lose the boots." Dawn winks and walks back toward her room.

As soon as she can breathe and move again, she scratches on Parker's door.

"Who is it?" A hoarse whisper.

"Parker, it's Nik. Lemme borrow your black Cons?"

Outside, she tapes the front door's lock, lets it close. She crouches in the bushes. The world is fragile and strange—lights off in the buildings, no one on the paths, no sounds. Security patrols the grounds through the night in an unmarked Taurus, sweeping a light over the hills, and she sees it now, playing over the cars in the West lot. She sprints behind Appleby, crosses Monroe Drive, and runs with her head down behind Summer. Nikki sits low in a hedge, panting, shaking. She's kneeling beneath a window, and wonders who's sleeping inside.

Her anger has already morphed into giddiness. Blackstick is lit up here and there, a checkerboard of insomnia. The older guys go to bed later. They sit around and wait for girls (who rarely arrive), take shots, smoke pot. High on Adderall, Ritalin, or coffee, depending on the weekly shipment. Watching porn on illegal TVs. Packing dips and sneaking cigarettes. Huffing computer cleaning fluid. Discussing existential queries. Strategizing. Bragging. Longing.

She runs the last leg and scratches the pane of the third basement window from the left.

It slides open. She lowers herself into darkness.

Diego is the son of Cubans who fled and then made it as club owners in Miami. *They're casually fabulous,* Nikki heard Schuyler say to Laine. Seth and Diego have been roommates since Prep year, and requested this basement room Senior year. No one could understand. It's dark and the laundry room's next door. Most years, the room's left for storage.

Seth hugs her; he's in a good mood. "I never thought you'd actually come over." He doesn't see the faint ink on her forehead since she scrubbed her face. He takes Nikki's hand and explains the location. The room gets little light, true, but is twice the size of regular rooms. Posters of old gangster movies plaster the walls, and the furniture is a weird clutter, much of it red Moroccan leather—donated by an eccentric aunt of Seth's who lives in New York City. The TV's cable wires are spliced to Mr. Hood's upstairs through the window. Diego is mixing a drink in the corner.

Seth and Diego aren't outsiders or freaks but aren't quite happy-go-lucky insiders anymore, either. They've done the Pair Revolution—it usually happens in the Upperform or Senior year. Most often it's roommates who stake out a territory—physical and metaphysical—and wage a quiet war from there against everything. This room is their territory. They have retreated from life at Wellington, and this is where they barricade themselves.

Nikki smiles, shakes her head as she looks around. *Unreal.*

"You want a drink?" Diego asks without looking up. He's wearing Calvin Klein briefs and purple socks, nothing else. Surround-sound speakers play The White Stripes.

"Yeah, sure. Hey, isn't the music loud?"

"The walls are soundproof because they didn't want the washer and dryer waking kids up," Seth replies. "Nik, check this out."

Nikki walks over to a cheap wading pool. *Do I explain what just happened to me?* A metal pipe tweaked out from under the floorboards is gushing steamy water into it.

"O my God!" Nikki laughs, her adrenaline raging.

"Diego and I read in an old yearbook that guys used to break open the floor of this dorm and use the hot water heater to fill up tubs like this. It's our own jacuzzi."

Diego hands Nikki a drink. "It's a Spiked Arnold Palmer. It's one of the best things I cribbed from these country club kids."

Nikki takes a sip. "Thanks, Diego. It's awesome."

Diego winks. "Cool. Okay, I'm headed upstairs. See you cats later."

Nikki and Seth sit on the couch, watching water fill the pink pool. Not knowing what to say, or how to say it, but looking at each other and looking away, grinning nervously. Nikki feels wasted, blind, but it's not the drink. It's this guy, this stolen night, this bizarre Wonderland vibe, the brutal event that just happened, and the delirium of having escaped the scene of the crime.

When the water nears the top, Seth cranks the pipe to stop the flow. It dribbles, then nothing. Nikki gets up and sticks a toe in—it's hot. Seth is at the makeshift bar fixing himself another cocktail, and when he stoops to pick up dropped ice cubes, she unbuttons her pants, drops her jeans, and slides off her top.

Nikki and Seth up to now have done very little besides kiss. They've kissed hard and long, till their lips were raw, and necks bruised, but that's almost it. There's been a lot of pressing and touching over clothes, a lot of dirty talking and hovering on the cliff. That Tuesday night, the night in question, they spent a half hour in the dark foyer of the chapel, standing up and making out, pressed against cold marble, woozy from it, unsteady by the time they parted.

But tonight could be more, could be enough, which is why Nikki is exhilarated, and why she's frightened. She unclasps her bra and peels it off, but leaves her thong.

It takes him a second, after taking in her almost-naked body, then after handing her the drink, to notice. Nikki looks away as he reads her skin. Then she gets brave enough to watch him take it in. His eyes nakedly register the words, and then their meaning, and then the meaning behind the meaning.

Strangely enough, this is a letter to him from Schuyler.

He hesitates, but she begs him with her eyes: *Fix this. Don't make me ask you to do whatever needs to be done. Figure it out and do it.* And he gets a ballpoint pen, without any further faltering. He starts to cross out the word on her breast, and worries that he's hurting her with the pen's tip.

"No, keep going," she says.

In his awkward, gangly, boy handwriting, he changes all the different insults to the same word: *Beautiful.*

They kiss forever, and keep kissing. They move onto the floor for what seems like hours.

Now Nikki's got her hands on his black mop of hair, and keeps wondering what the hell he's doing down there. Seth Walters is focused like a six-year-old boy head-deep in a bowl of Apple Jacks. Nikki decides to move things along and makes an escalating moan followed with a gentle tug of hair.

They stumble to the couch, trailing water on the floor. Nikki undoes Seth's Patagonia belt and unzips the J.Crew khakis, and is startled. The guys from home took pride in their grooming. They'd even half kid about how it made them look bigger. Nikki decides that must not be the way among preppy boys from the look of this wilderness.

Though Nikki has never actually reached orgasm, she's given plenty, and knows when he's almost ready. But then, without knowing she would do it, she pulls him into her.

"What?" he whispers, physically shocked.

And he's inside, where no one has ever been, and she lets him do what he's doing for about two strokes and she suddenly straightens like a board.

"Wait," she says, changing her mind. "I'm sorry."

"Okay, okay," he says, pulling out, his body trembling. "Okay."

When he comes, it's on her T-shirt, which is actually Laine's that Nikki borrowed without permission.

They get their breathing back in the dark. He asks if she's all right.

"Yeah, of course."

He eventually turns on a desk lamp and gets a tissue for himself. When he turns, he notices the stain. "Do you want me to get a towel?"

"Oh, sure, I guess. Do you have any club soda?"

"How 'bout Sprite?"

"Okay."

Nikki slides on her jeans, stuffs a thong in a pocket. She's light-headed. When he hands her the soda, she takes it without opening it. "I'll take care of it when I get back," she whispers.

"Why are you whispering?" he whispers.

She laughs a little. "I don't know."

"Are you taking off already?"

"Yeah, I am."

He's packing a dip. Then he touches her cheek. "I'm glad you came over, Nicole."

Walking back, she's not desperate and clandestine like she was on the way there. Tree branches clatter in the cool autumn night. Clouds move fast over the moon, changing the shadows, and light pools on the roofs. She saunters in the open, unafraid now of getting caught. She crosses the school grounds. She raises her arms as if they were wings, then lets them fall to her sides. Sometimes the body is the way out of the self. There's a big sky inside yourself where you can take flight. It's moments like these when she belongs to no one, not even herself. She is lost in some blue within or beyond or nearby, but not here.

10

The Lensks get pumpkins for Lancaster Four to carve. The girls sit outside the dorm one cool evening. Laine, Heather, and Schuyler are at Miss H's, so it's just the easy-going girls, or at least that's how Nikki thinks of it. On the picnic table are knives, spoons for scraping mush, paper towels. Mrs. Lensk tells them to save the seeds.

Their fingers get numb from being wet and cold. Nikki at one point tries to ball hers into a fist and cannot.

"Let me see yours," she says to Parker.

Parker's, of course, has flourishes: a Dalí mustache, sideburns, almond eyes.

Dawn is surprisingly deft and makes a loveably snaggle-toothed guy. Nik keeps lamenting that her own is boring, so Mr. Lensk appraises it.

"That's what my mother would have called an honest face," he finally pronounces.

Aya talks to Nikki about Laine; asks if they've become friends. Her black hair shines in the twilight.

"Umm," Nikki says, working to get the last bits of pumpkin out of the cavity. "Not really. We've just decided to, I dunno. Do our own thing."

They sit in the Lensks' apartment later and watch old *Addams Family* episodes, eat the just-roasted pumpkin seeds, and drink sparkling cider. When they look out the window, their civilization of grinning and winking and laughing heads blooms with orange light, and those faces cast long fluid wavering golden shapes on the lawn.

Halloween. Nikki dresses in Parker's room, since she's been avoiding Laine as much as possible, and the two girls share a backstage excitement. Parker's settled on Patti Smith from the cover of *Horses*, having abandoned Annie Hall. Nikki, after considering a hundred options, is going to be a Princess, which is most Halloweens.

Parker sews sequins onto the T-shirt Nikki's wearing. Nikki came to the room unadorned and has been decorated with tulle, satin, spangles, silk flowers, and charms, like a Christmas tree, standing with her arms out and just waiting, giggling, to be pricked by the needle.

Parker, standing back now and considering her work,

says, "Let's have fun tonight."

"What did you say?" Nikki asks, incredulous.

Parker takes the sewing needle from between her teeth. "Let's have fun tonight."

"No, I heard you." Nikki laughs. "I just never thought that would come out of your mouth."

"I'm a rock star tonight, come on."

"Should we be *bad*?" Nikki says, tasting her own delicious words as she says them.

Parker gets a look that is equal parts sparked interest and reluctance. "Let's play it by ear," she says.

"Don't worry, Park, I'm not asking you to sign a contract or something."

It's been raining all day but it's tapered off. They walk through the lamplit dark to the student center, the wet earth reeking of decomposition—in a good, invigorating way. Nikki holds up her pink crinoline skirt so she doesn't kick mud back onto it. The night is extremely quiet, the way it is after a heavy rain.

Shortly after they leave the building, Schuyler peeks in to say hi to Laine, her features arranged in casual innocence. Laine, who hates Halloween, is dressed as a field hockey player. In her own uniform. She gapes at Schuyler.

"What?" Schuyler asks in feigned ignorance.

"Wow, that's . . ."

"Not bad, right? Listen, can I see that necklace?"

Schuyler points to a gold chain pooled on Nikki's desk.

Laine stands in place, looks at the necklace. "Why?" she asks finally, stalling.

"I just want to see it."

Laine finally and slowly, as if dragging feet through honey, gets the jewelry and hands it over, coiling it into Schuyler's palm. Schuyler puts it on.

"What are you doing?" Laine says.

"Just seeing how it looks." Schuyler makes a serious face in the mirror, turns this way and that. "Awesome."

As Schuyler starts to go, Laine panics. "Hold on, Schuyler."

"What?" Schuyler asks, slipping through the door.

"Hold on," Laine says without meaning, without conviction, without effect.

The movie is *The Shining*, and the dark auditorium chants *All work and no play makes Jack a dull boy*. Parker and Nik were late to the film so when the crowd emerges they're overwhelmed by the transformation. No more student body. Just a random gang of cowgirls, Dick Cheney, Grandmaster Flash, French maids, cross-dressers, cheerleaders, Courtney Love, and soldiers.

Everyone lounges around the student center, invigorated by a sense of alias. Someone throws candy corns into someone's mouth across the room, or at least aims. Nikki sees Chase, Greg, Gabriel, and Noah dressed like STDs, a trick cribbed from a Dave Chappelle skit.

"You guys look amazing!" she says.

Noah, who's dressed as gonorrhea, pretends to be bashful. "Yeah, I know."

"That's so attractive, venereal diseases. Great for business, right? You guys definitely know how to get girls."

The guys laugh roughly, and get quiet.

The haunted house was created by theater set design and art students in the back of the center. It's got a David Lynch flavor this year. Parker, who helped make it, still has to hold Nikki's hand as they walk through the tiny paint-fuming, dizzy-making maze. Suddenly a red strobe light flickers on a film still of *Psycho* taped to the wall, and there's a recording of a scream over a real news anchor reporting a murder in Connecticut. Both girls squeal, mainly because it feels good.

They're in a room with glowing blood splattered on walls, listening to a recitation of Charles Manson, when Nikki asks Parker why she doesn't go for Diego tonight.

"I don't know. He's just too . . . abrupt. Or forthright."

"He's not some junkie jazz musician who died in the fifties, that's why you don't like him. Be honest."

"That's deep."

"Just be nice to him, could you do that?"

After the haunted house, they waste time with everyone

else in the lounge. Nikki keeps asking people who Parker is, and they shrug. "See, no one has any clue."

"They should, it's an *iconic* image."

"Well, sweetheart, they don't."

Parker stamps her feet. "No! I just have to get into position."

She leans against the wall in her white button-down shirt with a tie thrown around her neck, men's pants wrinkled, jacket thrown over her shoulder. Nikki decides Parker looks slinky, sexy like this—metamorphosis becomes her. Jorgen walks by.

"Patti Smith, *Horses*. That's cool, Parker."

Nikki's trying to make people kneel at her feet with her wand, getting little success but much attention, when Seth and Diego roll in, hands in pockets. Seth's face is vague; he's always less attractive when he's fucked up. And more attractive for being less attractive by being fucked up.

"On your knees boy." Nikki waves her stick, glitter drifting after it through the air.

Seth doesn't take his hands out of his pockets or stand up from leaning against the newspaper racks. "Yeah, I don't think so."

Neither guy is wearing a costume. Parker asks what they are.

"Apathy," Diego says.

"That's retarded," Nikki says.

"Okay, princess. What are you, eight?"

"Ha ha," Nikki says and reaches for Seth's Coke can because she's thirsty, not thinking. "Can I get a sip?"

"You'll get more than a sip. Sure you want that?"

Nikki and Parker trade looks. And grin. When they take sips, it makes them drunk immediately—not chemically but psychologically. It's the taste of misbehavior. Nikki and Parker huddle and whisper about nothing, feeling sexily subversive. Diego refills in the men's room, where they've stashed the bottle of Beam in the toilet tank. When he comes out, he suggests the four of them walk to the woods.

Nikki and Parker do their telepathic communication again.

"Sure," Nikki says.

Diego and Seth start out, tell the girls to wait five minutes. Nikki and Parker sip punch and eat orange-iced cookies, tapping their feet and trading meaningful stares. They're both exalted, made superior by the touch of liquor in their blood and their impending destination. At exactly five minutes they stroll down the hall.

A group approaches but Nikki doesn't see who it is until it's too late.

That's me.

Schuyler's wearing skintight jeans, heeled boots, and a white hoodie with SOUTH BEACH written on it in marker and the zipper pulled down too far, something plumping up her bra to absurd proportion, her face deranged by makeup. Schuyler nonchalantly pops a chocolate into her mouth.

"What are you?" Nikki says with flat accusation.

Schuyler turns to Heather, who's dressed similarly but without specific references to Nikki. They both shrug. "We're, like, just girls from Long Island. Or we could even be girls from Jersey or somewhere. I'm Bridge and she's Tunnel, babe."

The crew laughs. As they do Nikki sees a sparkle on Schuyler's neck. It's Nikki's necklace, the one she's had forever. The two charms hanging, the Chai and the cross. Representing her mother and father.

"You stole that!" Nikki shrieks.

Even Parker is alarmed. Everyone talks at once, trying to get Nikki to be quiet as she repeats over and over: "You stole that from my room! You fucking stole that!"

Schuyler keeps trying to say something. Nikki talks over her.

"You went into my room and fucking *took* that! That is stealing."

"*Excuse* me," Schuyler finally shouts and all are silent. "Maybe you should talk to your roommate about that. Seriously. Before you open your little mouth *one more time* and tell me what I did. Okay? And please, take this thing. It's not like it cost a fortune, my dear, so you don't need to have an ulcer."

Nikki has the feeling, not for the first time, that she's outmatched. It doesn't tame her fury, it just sends her looking for Laine. Parker runs after her, trying to get her jacket on as they run outside.

Laine is in the common room of the dorm with two other girls dressed as field hockey players, spread out on the couch with water bottles and caramel apples, watching *Rosemary's Baby* on TV. Laine sees Nikki's face and her own face falls. She gets up but doesn't know what to do next.

Nikki holds up the chain.

"She took it," Laine says.

"She took it or you gave it to her?"

"She took it, but—"

"But what? What?"

Laine looks away, her hands on her hips. The moon is so minor the window is black.

"Did she ask you for it? Because I'm going to turn her in, I'm going to—"

Laine looks with horror. "Don't do that."

"Why not, because you like her, or because you fucking gave this to her?"

Laine pauses for just a moment. "I let her take it."

"That's the same as giving it to her. Isn't it?"

"I don't know," Laine says earnestly.

"Aw, screw that. You know."

The end of the night on Lancaster Four is a soap opera. Girls go room to room, like bees into tunnels of a hive. Comforting, debating, accusing. Nikki's holed up in her den, tears streaking her cheeks, princess outfit torn and lying on the floor. Schuyler holds court in her own room. Laine hides in the common room, trying to hear what people are saying without looking like she's doing that.

Nikki is going to tell the Lensks about Laine, but Parker ultimately points to Nikki's mouth.

"What?" Nikki says scornfully.

"You've got bourbon on your breath," Parker says apologetically.

That night candy wrappers blow over the grounds, get caught in hedges' roots. They'll be picked out by morning, the maintenance staff anticipating this litter. Laine and Nikki lie in their beds, Laine having snuck in after Nikki turned off the light, Nikki waiting for Laine to say something, Laine trying to say something and trying to say something, on and on in disorienting spurts of insomnia, into the silvery, freezing morning.

A shimmering Sunday. The sky is turquoise and mean, the trees finally bare. Seth and Nikki trudge through pine and hardwood forest. Alongside, a creek trickles over boulders. They avoid the trails and main cabins for fear of teachers. Occasionally they pause when they hear twigs snap; it's an added thrill.

When she's with him, Nikki is able to forget that life at Wellington hasn't evened out, and she exists in the moment. In his pocket, Seth has a Nick Drake tape for the relic of a transistor radio in Kingston—the barest-boned and least-known cabin nearby.

In these far-ranging woods, the network of trails and cabins is vast. Rebellious students built most of the cabins decades ago and named them Maggie's Farm, Brokedown Palace, Havana, Amsterdam, Exile on Main Street, and Kingston. Their locations are passed down like treasure and appreciated more for solitude than scenery. Their walls are carved with initials, lyrics, first loves, axioms, desperate crushes, war cries, and war protests, and the ceiling darkened by smoke and resin.

"Are we going much farther?" Nikki whines, just to talk.

"Easy, Nicky Hilton, we'll be there in a second. You want me to carry you?" He walks ahead holding branches and pointing out vines.

"Yo, *who's* Nicky Hilton? I *shingle*, okay?"

Kingston is nothing more than a shed on the edge of a summer home property. A vintage red velvet loveseat sits in front of a man-made fire pit. This is the cabin for the true alternatives, the older ones, kids who like nature but litter the cabin with cigarette butts and bottle tops, the angry ones. Seth uncaps a can of spray paint and adds to the wall:

Come in, she said, I'll give you shelter from the storm . . .

Nikki has brought one rolled cigarette, compliments of Parker, and Seth strikes a lighter for her. He pats the cushion next to him.

"Pretty sweet place, huh?"

Nikki nods. "Yeah, it's awesome."

"Chase's brother Reed showed me this cabin before he graduated. No one really knows where it is, so you never get bothered. Just feels like Wellington is so distant out here, ya know?"

Nikki is dizzy from smoking and spray paint, and giggles at everything Seth says. Holding her cigarette far away, she leans to bite his ear. This is before foreplay, the pre-pregame. She picks an eyelash off his cheek and blows it away with a wish. She pretends to think about it seriously—"I wish . . . Seth wouldn't eat Mexican before hooking up with me."

"Dude, I'm chewing gum, for you." He takes out the white gob and shows her.

"Not good enough," she says, and they push and pull each other, play wrestling. He takes the cigarette then, and grinds it with his boot on the dirt floor.

Nikki leans in to Seth and starts kissing his neck. She pulls away and smiles.

"What?" he asks.

"Nothing. So tell me how you two got together."

It takes him a moment to figure out who she means, but then he growls with reluctance. "C'mon, you don't want to go there, Nik, and I would *honestly* just as soon forget."

"Please, please, pretty please? Just tell me how you hooked up."

Seth sighs, stares at the ceiling, blows his bangs. "This is stupid."

Nikki nuzzles his cheek, purring. Seth finally admits they hooked up on Valentine's Day last year. "And it was fun."

Nikki stares at him, stormy-eyed.

"Not that fun," he rushes to amend, realizing that joke will go nowhere. "I don't know, the girl's all drama. It's fun for like two seconds. It's a whirlwind, it's crazy. But like, I couldn't keep track of when she was mad or why and when she was in love and wanted to go get hitched in Vegas. She was shooting at my feet, right? Making me dance. Holy shit, her parents built a *monster*."

"Who dumped who?"

"We went to Stowe, and she got wasted one night, was all over this kid Clay. This total dick."

"So you broke up with her."

"Well, we fought."

Nikki's dissatisfied that he didn't officially kick Schuyler to the curb. She traces his jaw with her finger. "Was she good?" she asks slyly.

Seth looks at her with interest and amusement. "You're bad."

"Was she?" Nikki teases.

"Are you really asking me that?"

No, baby. If you knew girls at all, you would know I'm asking if you love me.

He runs his hand over her—over her shirt with his thumb—and she catches her breath. His eyes are wet, and he looks her up and down, urgent and drowsy at the same time. She slides one lazy leg between his thighs, blue jeans on blue jeans, and his fingers spread wide across her back, pressing her to him so hard it almost hurts.

A knock sends them both reeling back on the couch. "Oh, shit!" Seth whispers.

Nikki looks at his white face. They both look at the door.

Before they can kick away the cigarette butt or paint can, the door swings open.

Dean Talliworth stands in the doorway like a general discovering AWOL soldiers. Somehow, in wingtips, he's tracked them through thick forest to this cabin. Perhaps he saw them strolling across fields and followed the scent like an old English setter on a hunt. Or maybe he was tipped off by some soulless student.

"Well, well . . . Mr. Walters. I wish I could be surprised to see you here. Considering you were slated for detention one hour ago." He picks up the cigarette butt and pockets it. "I suggest you both leave now. You first, Ms. Olivetti. I would like a word with Mr. Walters."

Nikki turns to say good-bye to Seth, but he waves her away. His eyes are glazed and distant.

11

ean Talliworth's office dead-ends Swallow Wing, next to Admissions. His secretary has Nikki waiting in a chintz armchair in the lobby. Normally, being caught fooling around or off campus just accords one a slash, as opposed to drinking or drug violations, which will get you booted, so she's praying that's all she gets.

A man and woman are sipping coffee, talking quietly. They don't know each other and Nikki surmises they're waiting for children getting interviewed for admittance.

"Well, did you hear about Kaiyoh? It's Japan's first Eton-style prep school."

"*Really?* I don't believe I have." The woman is elegant in a black suit, black tights and heels, a black ponytail, rose lipstick, a cup and saucer balanced on her knee.

"Yup, that's right. They even had the director of Eton consult. I guess they're concerned about producing leaders with character, which they used to produce effortlessly. But they feel that the *capacity* has, I don't know, been swallowed up by competitive schooling, exams. They want to locate that well-rounded, moral individual."

"Wellington, prep schools in general, I *think* are based on such a model, no?"

"Yup," the man in the corduroy jacket says, his dark blond hair standing up in a sporty, confident way. "And throw in some military. You know, break 'em down, break 'em all down to humble, and then you got yourself the power to build 'em up the way you want. Because they need the reward of your support and such."

The woman shakes her head slowly, smiling. "Strange, isn't it? Now, how old is yours?"

"He's thirteen. Yup, Gerald's thirteen. And yours?"

"Kira's fifteen."

The secretary stands and beckons. As Nikki crosses the plush rug, the secretary catches her eye and smiles, follows Nikki without blinking.

"Come in." Dean Talliworth's faux English accent resonates in the wood-paneled room after Nikki knocks.

"Uh, Dean Talliworth? I got a note in my, my, uh, mailbox to see you," Nikki is stuttering.

Randolph Talliworth turns his large frame to face her.

When she entered he was facing the window. Just staring. *Maybe it's intimidation. What a freak.*

"Ah yes, Miss Olivetti." Her name sounds dirty the way he pronounces it: Oli-*vetti*. "Well, Nicole, we have a situation on our hands, don't we? Would you please sit?"

Nikki perches on the brown leather couch.

"First off let me ask—are you enjoying your time here at Wellington?"

Nikki's caught off guard. *What does he mean, enjoying? Is this a trick question? Ew, I hate this.* "Um, yeah. I mean, I really enjoy my classes. I've met some nice people. And look, I am *really* sorry about what happened in the woods. It was just a dumb decision. I hope you won't judge me solely on that."

"I appreciate your candor, Nicole. I am also *pleased* to hear that you are enjoying your experience thus far. You know, the transition can be rather unsettling. New environment, new standards, higher expectations—these things overwhelm students at times. I am glad you are adjusting so well, my dear."

He reviews some notes he's made on a yellow legal pad, bifocals edged to the tip of his nose. "Now, Nicole, let me first preface this by saying that this is in no way an attack on you as a person, your upbringing, or your intentions."

"O-*kay*," she says slowly.

"It has come to my attention that some of the faculty,

and students as well, are concerned about your *behavior*. I am not referring to the cabin incident, though that has not helped the matter. It seems, however, that you may have, whether justifiably or not, garnered an unfortunate reputation. Are you following me?"

Nikki nods haltingly.

"Here at Wellington we try to prepare you in all facets of life. Nicole, right now we are concerned that you may be hanging out with certain people. Seth Walters and Diego Caroles, for example, are not good influences at this juncture. Do you understand?"

Dean Talliworth hesitates briefly, then continues. "We also ask that you *cease* the promiscuous behavior and dress. Quite frankly, your attire has made some of the student body, and faculty, rather uncomfortable."

Nikki suddenly feels her sexual parts glow red through her clothes, and crosses her legs and folds her arms. This is not because he's looking at her body, but because he's forcing himself *not* to look, and to stare in an increasingly demented way at her face. This feels worse than if he dragged his gaze from her head to her toes.

"Nicole, I think it is only fair to tell you that we have also sent a letter home to your parents regarding our concerns. It only outlines what we have discussed here and nothing more. Is there anything you should like to ask me?"

She stares, speechless.

"I mean, I feel that you work to act the part of a tough girl"—and here he lifts himself from his chair enough to imitate something she supposes is a tough girl's strut, but he looks like a chicken pecking seed—"but that doesn't mean you cannot come to us with your emotional issues. We are *good* listeners, you may very well be surprised! Now. *Do* you have anything you would like to ask me at this point, Nicole?"

Gee. Hmmm. Let me think. Do I have anything to ask? Yeah, I guess I'd love to know if I SHOVE THAT TYPHOID YEL-LOW RIBBON THAT'S TIED AROUND YOUR TURKEY NECK UP YOUR MICROSCOPICALLY TIGHTENED ASS, WOULD THE WELLINGTON CREST COME OUT OF YOUR MOUTH?

"Nicole?"

"Oh, I'm sorry. No, I have no questions."

"Nicole, we think you have a lot of potential and want to see you *succeed* here."

Nikki nods her head, mumbles. Somehow makes it out the door before those hot, simmering, vicious tears well over. If the woman in black had been in the waiting room, Nikki would have flung herself on her lap and bawled. But she's gone.

Laine taps on the glass of Miss Hartford's office. Miss H,

on the phone, motions Laine inside. Algebra books on the desk, field hockey pictures, playbooks, Dartmouth banners. A putty ball grip strengthener. Miss Hartford mouths to Laine to sit.

"Okay. Got it. Bye." Miss Hartford hangs up. "Thanks for coming by. How was lunch?"

Laine notices two Division I All-American certificates hanging. "It was fine."

"We're running double suicides today. We're going to step up conditioning drills this week. The team looked fatigued against Deerfield, don't you think?"

Laine processes what she had for lunch—*whole-wheat toast, one banana, peanuts for protein. It should stay down.*

"Yeah, I guess," she agrees.

"I thought so. Listen, Laine, I'm going to cut to the chase here."

The office suddenly feels smaller. "Okay."

"During the teacher conference, there was chatter about your roommate. And let me just say, in these meetings, chatter is not good, especially for someone so new at school. What I'm getting at here, I want you to feel you can *tell* me if rooming with her is too much."

"Okay. But actually, we barely see each other."

"Well, that's good. 'Cause you see, when someone gets a reputation early on, it's an *uphill* climb. You know, I don't think anyone knows this, so mum's the word. But Jinny

Mitchell in Admissions let Nicole Olivetti into the school. And it was on the recommendation of a board member. Well, we find out at this meeting last week the board member is *married* to Nikki's shrink, and that they're both bleeding heart *liberals*, and I honestly think it's a cruel joke on their part. To get this poor girl into this place where she doesn't belong."

Miss H's eyes glow, and Laine realizes she likes the scandal. Laine pulls at her turtleneck.

"Do you understand? They're *undermining* the principles of this place. I don't know. Jinny did some digging, and we're all just flabbergasted. But it does help explain what's happening. And it means you *don't* need to feel bad if you want, for example, a room transfer."

Miss H is not offering this option, but suggesting it. And Laine is overwhelmed by this woman's protectiveness, her fervor in nurturing Laine. Her meticulous and unrelenting attention to Laine's body, lifestyle, comfort, and situation.

"Wow, maybe that would be a good idea," Laine says. Cutting Nikki out of her life is, frankly, appealing. *Although it would be public, and people would ask questions.* "Let me sleep on it, is that cool?"

"Of course, Laine. I want to throw it out there, that's all. See you at practice."

Laine heads toward the door.

"There is one other thing," Miss H says. "It's not just faculty I'm hearing this from."

Laine nods. *It doesn't take much to figure out which field hockey captains could be bad-mouthing Nikki.*

Laine gets a box with a Michigan return address that afternoon. Dried cherries from her dad. She tastes one, remembers trips to the lakes, fishing with him, drinking Cokes out in the boat, picking cherries.

She has strange feelings about having taken on Miss H as her family. She almost feels like the coach is *replacing* her parents. And with such severe affection.

Lord knows, Dad wasn't severe. He was messy and ridiculous. He had funny and superfluous objects tucked into his pockets: a magnifying glass he used to look at flowers, a weathered field guide to birds of the Pacific Northwest (only handy if he was on the East Coast), a blue hankie with which he wiped ice cream off kids' faces or smeared condensation off the inner windshield of the car.

In the glove box, he kept a first-aid box—in it was a tiny bottle of Dewar's, spreadable cheese, Triscuits, seltzer, raisins, and one butterscotch candy. The girls thought it was hysterical and made him open it all the time.

"Yeah, who's that going to save, Tommy? Yourself, that's all," Polly would mutter.

Where once she saw humor, Laine began to think of the

kit as a hot spot, a stepping stone to dissolution. But now, looking back, she thinks it's funny all over again. *I miss him. I really miss him.*

Nikki sees Laine carrying a box from the mailroom and idly wonders what she got. *Not like she'll share.* Nikki had called Ness and blubbered after the Talliworth meeting, and today she gets a pink envelope covered in bad doodles with a Plainview return address. *That sweet little bitch!* Nikki is laughing now. She tears the envelope to read the notebook paper.

> *Hey Slut . . . Just checking on you baby girl. I am so stupid bored in Algebra right now, it is KILLING me. Tyson skipped class. I think he got stoned with Mikey at lunch and went to the new Vin Diesel movie. So how is your senior boy-toy? Speaking of, I hooked up with Mikey last week. I went down on him and he tasted like Versace cologne and sour milk—GROSS!! I assume you don't care, I know you had a cruuussshhh, but now you got a preppy hot & sticky studhorse of yer own. I want one! & my birthday's comin up, wink wink. OH! You'll love this—Jay Brillstein is gay!! Yeah, can you believe it? He rubbed up on Steve's piece at Mikey's house last weekend. Crazy, right!? Steve beat the shit out of him, but now everyone's chill. Not like we didn't*

*know already right? Anyway, good news—party at
the skate park t-giving . . . it will be your homecoming!! Oh, shit, the bell just rang. Got to meet the crew
at lunch. Call soon.*

Love ya, bitch. Ness

Nikki sits on a black leather couch and rereads the letter. She misses Ness. She misses cologne, nights out, sipping from a pint in the cold, huddled with friends, coming
home from school to Sharon's lasagna baking, going to the
movies in someone's new car, kicking it with her girls in
someone's bedroom. For the first time, Nikki lets herself
imagine withdrawing from this place. She pictures a white
flag. *I'm done here. You got me. Good for you, motherfuckers.*

12

A scratch on the door, and Laine's stomach turns. 5:12 A.M. *Not again.* She drags herself in boxers and long-john shirt and opens it, expecting to see Schuyler with whip and gag this time.

It's a girl she's never seen before, in a beige suede cowboy jacket and a baseball hat turned backward.

"I'm Trevor's girlfriend," the girl says quietly. "He asked me to get you, he's not allowed in here."

Laine stares at this girl, wondering if she's dreaming. She doesn't know a Trevor.

"Sage is foaling. If you want to come, we'll drive you down."

Oh Jesus. Laine does the math: If it's dawn, is this cruising? Is this sneaking out at night, or getting up really early?

It doesn't matter. She drags jeans and a sweater on, grabs her coat and newsboy cap. Nikki looks up blurrily, perhaps still asleep, and Laine tells her she'll be right back.

She thanks the girl as they head down the stairs but the girl doesn't respond.

The moon is huge and gold like a pear, outrageous in the cold black sky. Trevor leans out his truck window and asks, in hushed voice, if she minds them getting her up. She vehemently shakes her head.

"No, I'm glad, thank you."

They bump, three across the front seat, in Trevor's Chevy to the stable. A white-haired woman in paddock boots, a vet, beckons them into the barn, where Sage has a cleanly strawed stall. Sage is lying down, sweating. Trevor tells Laine that she's been restless, and had wax on her teats yesterday, so they thought this was coming.

There is a hush as the animal works. Suddenly the sac breaks and spills, and they all look at one another. The ethic in foaling is no interference; the mare can usually deliver with no injury if people stay out of the way. There's iodine and instruments at the ready, but hopefully Sage won't need it.

Two front hooves appear, and then the nose of the foal between the knees. *It is diving out of its mother, into the world.* The membrane on its face breaks. Outside, the sky goes violet at the edges, and Sage pushes hard, and again, straining.

There is some concern after fifteen minutes, but then she exerts herself one last time, and her foal slips out.

It's a colt, and he lies stunned in straw for ten minutes before he nickers to his mother. Sage starts licking his hide, and the stall is dense with joy and awe and relief, as well as the odors of birth, struggle, placenta.

"Cheers!" Everyone clinks Dixie cups of orange juice.

Laine walks slowly back to school. The sun is rising white above the buildings. Ferns turn yellow at their edges with the morning light. The miracle of life is a phrase that's always made her want to barf. *But what else just happened back there?* That animal, that soul, came into the world just now. He didn't use to exist. While she watched, he *became.*

She twists her cap backward and walks with hands in pockets. High on this idea, and on the primeval fumes of delivery, she considers for the first time the fact that she wasn't always alive. This is the reverse of imagining one's death.

Woods Crew. Air that will not move, hanging over everyone with icy malevolence. The gang is happy to pile into the truck as gray twilight begins, and to huddle.

Nikki sees a bunny spasm away from the vehicle into the darkness. "Oh my God, I want to wrap that little thing up! Put him in a blanket and take it home, make it better."

Grant laughs. "You continue to come up with the greatest, most farfetched material, dear Nicole. I should never die in the woods for lack of amusement if you're with us. But I must ask you what on earth you want to save the bunny from? His natural life? He's content. He's what he's supposed to be. It's a happiness that is simple and inevitable, Nicole."

"Yeah, yeah." In the confusion of dusk and trees beyond, Nicole wonders if the thing moving could be Seth in a blackwatch jacket. She strains to see. *It's definitely a guy, isn't it, yes it is. It's him* . . . She yearns after the vanishing figure.

Grant continues to preach. "Although, I was in Wyoming last year, and when there should have been snow, the snow-rabbits turned white to conceal themselves from predators, as they always have. But due to global warming and all that foul tragedy, there was no snow. So the white bunnies stood out on the dark plains like candy to the hawks, who just picked them up like it was *nothing.*"

Grant says "nothing" a couple more times, still amazed after a year.

Nikki likes to visit Parker in the art room in the evenings. Years before, Wellington had acquired an old farm next to the campus, and these outbuildings are now printmaking rooms and dance spaces and art studios. Tonight, Parker and Greg draw, listening to Mos Def. Their easels in front of a table covered by white paper pulled from a roll. They study a still life.

A conch shell.

In a smoky vase, a mess of hot pink wild roses, red mums, fir tips, and birch twigs.

A wooden *B* from a kid's toy set.

A glass milk bottle.

An antique shirt, once white but now cream, on a hanger that dangles from a ceiling pipe.

The assignment is Light. The teacher asked the class to investigate each object here, each one made of a different material, the molecules hanging together in different patterns, allowing light to pass through or reflect off of it in unique ways. *Light,* she claimed, *is at the center of most experience, and subsequently most art.*

Nikki moves restlessly around the studio. All afternoon she looked for Seth, even daring to ask people if they'd seen him. Rory Winchester looked her in the eye and said, "Maybe he's out at Kingston. Heard he spends a lot of time there." Heather had been near and stifled a laugh. Parker even commented on his recent scarcity. Now Nikki studies Greg's drawing with her arms crossed, his conch shell obscured by eraser rubouts.

"It's so bad," he says, bandit tucked under lip. He hasn't come to stomach straight tobacco like Noah and Chase, so the packet is perfect.

"No, it's a nice beginning," Nikki says.

"You don't know shit about it, girl," he says. "Ha ha,

wait till *you* got to fill your art requirement. You'll be down here for hours, messing with a bunch of shells and flowers and whatever."

Parker butts in. "Greg, you're down here more than you have to be."

"What are you saying?" he squeals.

"I think you like it."

"I don't know. Maybe it's not so bad. I used to draw comic book heroes over and over again for my mother. Doing this kind of reminds me of that."

Nikki likes it in here, too. Outside, dried-out lavender shivers in the deep blue evening, blossoms crusty and dropping seeds. Next door in the printmaking studio two older kids in aprons make each other laugh hysterically. All these small structures look onto a path that runs between classrooms and the gym, and suddenly Laine hurries by outside in a baby-blue coat and Keds.

"There goes my dear friend," Nikki says, pressing her nose to the window.

"Yeah, you live with her right? That girl . . . ," Greg says. "Shit."

"What?" Parker prompts.

"It sounds messed up. I don't know. Lots of people are fine with her. I just think the girl's so stuck up."

Parker and Nikki look at each other.

"She's kind of dead, like . . ." Greg is looking at his drawing again; he pretends to be a master and mimes a final brush stroke to be done. He doesn't realize he's said anything substantial about Laine. He walks over to see Parker's. "See! Look at your milk bottle, girl. Look at the *liiigggghhhttt.*"

He picks up one of the flashlights they're using for this project, points it into his mouth. Nikki giggles, turns off the overheads. They play games, turning their cheeks molten apricot, or shining the lamp through their hands to see the bones.

"This is stupid." Greg laughs, but continues, making a strobe by covering and uncovering the flashlight. "We may as well mess around while we can. We got a matter of hours before this place is full up with parents putting they noses everywhere. Are you girls ready?"

"I don't think it's something you can get ready for." Nikki laughs.

Parker takes this opportunity to sharpen her pencil. She clears her throat but doesn't answer. Everyone's got a *bundle* of feelings regarding Parents' Weekend, not all of them good.

24–17. Hotchkiss leads Wellington as the third quarter begins.

"Black fella down there can run, can't he!" Randall "Rocket" Dobbs stands on sidelines in a red blazer, a South Carolina flag embroidered bow tie, and wide butter-yellow cords.

Parents' Weekend is kicked off by the "Friday Night Lights" Homecoming football game. Boarding school football is a tennis-shoe league to the outside world, but that hasn't stopped Wellington from investing $40K into lights and Astroturf. Rocket Dobbs played on this field forty-seven years ago, when it was raw dirt, and never hides contempt for his boys who haven't pursued the sport. Today he luxuriates in the memories this sunny, brisk afternoon revives.

"Jesus, Dad, keep your voice down." Chase sits beneath his father who yells "hit him" every other play, slamming balled fist into palm and growling like a tiger, then smiling at his son. The accent, the bawdy jokes—it seemed normal among friends and family, but this is slow death, having this wild beast among new peers.

Nikki looks at Chase, his hand over his eyes. It's been interesting, watching Chase and Greg grapple with the suitcases of ideas, about being white and being black, they each brought to Wellington. She's overheard heated banter, jokes taken too far—exchanges that end in sharp words, slammed doors. Silence for a day, a night. Chase is closer to Greg than to anyone else at this point but doesn't recognize his own inherited disposition: He feels, in some way, he's doing Greg a favor by being open-minded, or generous, as a white guy with a black guy for a best friend. Nikki sees now who might have handed *that* one down. Greg, fast to anger, cuts Chase to the core, ridiculing him for being a legacy, stating that he'll never know what he's capable of since he's got that silver spoon hanging out of his mouth. Greg says things he can't unsay, and often does so with as many people around to overhear as possible.

But those two always mend it, their tie made stronger by the process, whatever it takes.

"Hey, Nik—who're your friends?" Victor Olivetti asks. "Any of them here?"

Nikki points to Chase, and Gabriel, who's sitting with him. When Chase grimaces at his father's hollering, Gabriel grins.

"Yeah, Daddy—those are a couple of my friends. Chase is the tall blond, and the guy in the peacoat is Gabriel." Nikki leans back against his chest as the fourth quarter begins.

Victor stands out in the sea of tweed, blazers, khaki. His black suit and black turtleneck hug his bear chest. Sharon talks on her cell until Victor gestures to walk behind the bleachers so she won't disturb the fans. She mouths "Sorry" and stands as the ball is hiked.

Randall Dobbs yells: "Down in front!"

Sharon turns with a scowl. "Oh, ease up, it's only high school."

Nikki watches Greg. The game ended, 27–24. Greg fumbled on the final drive. Hotchkiss is victorious. The players shake hands at midfield. Greg never moves, isolated in a circle of failure. His helmet remains fastened.

"Well, that's too bad. That number seven played a hell of a game. Where's he going to college?" Victor asks as people in the bleachers disperse.

"He's only a sophomore, Daddy. He's a friend of mine, also. He grew up in Brooklyn, like you."

"Oh, yeah? Very nice."

"Yeah. . . ."

"Where's Laine? That's her name, right?"

"Uh, probably with her parents somewhere."

"You good?" Victor looks sideways at Nikki.

"Yeah, yeah." Nikki is torn between wanting to tell her dad she's been kicked in the face by this place and wanting to show the place off. She wants his comfort *and* his respect. This is why she never tells him anything in her calls home.

"So I'll meet you back here for the 'Headmaster Tea,'" Nikki says in an English accent, and they laugh.

"Sounds bloody *lovely*, my *dear*. I'll go put on my knickers and be back."

"We're so proud of our Lainey." Cynthia Ryan, the Headmaster's wife, smiles crinkle-eyed at Laine. "She's made quite the impression on the fields."

In fact, this is only Laine and Cynthia's second meeting.

The first was during the interview last year when Cynthia "dropped by" Admissions to say hello—and was *oh so surprised* to see Philip Breck with his daughter, and his kajillions of dollars.

Parents and kids mill about the living room of the Headmaster's house, making cocktail talk minus cocktails. A fire snaps and crackles, birch logs turning black. Dining Hall staff wander with starched aprons, offering refills of weak tea. The gathering is ostensibly a traditional way for parents to interact with the Headmaster and his wife, but the Ryans aren't really meeting anyone new, instead mingling with old friends and big donors. Cynthia has a telekinetic way of bossing around her husband that's in high force presently.

On display in the living room: a first edition of *A Separate Peace*, a Wellington crest oar, an Andrew Wyeth watercolor, Shaker furniture, a framed page of Coltrane's notes for *Kind of Blue*—shares bought of the intellect, investments in humanity at large.

Laine looks around and decides that if someone traded these portraits of past headmasters with the portraits at the Round Hill Club, no one would notice. These are like her metaphysical grandfathers, always peering from above, judging her.

Nikki sees Parker enter the room with her mom and her Ichabod Crane father, who stoops under the ceiling beam.

Her dad has a gold eagle earring in one ear and his wedding ring is a tattoo around his finger. He stands behind his wife, whose brown-silver hair is as long as Parker's. His face is waxy and pinched, and he lets Mrs. Cole do the talking. Nikki has never seen Parker so uneasy, until another apprehensive family is drawn to them like a magnet and they all talk and relax, even the dad. Nikki understands now who Parker means when she talks about loving a crazy person.

Nikki introduces herself to the Coles, drags Parker to do a lap. Parents' Weekend sometimes catapults a loser into fame if they have a hot brother or sister, and that's what happens now with Baroness Greta von Something-something, who is standing next to a 6'2" golden-haired young buck of a brother—with a rosebud mouth and mean, decadent, deviant eyes.

"OHmyGOD, that kid, don't let him near me," Nikki says into Parker's ear.

"Why?"

"I'm kidding. That boy could WRECK me in under a minute."

The guy senses the stares and turns, his eyes flashing but lips unmoved.

"He's evil hot," Nikki mutters, swooning.

Guys, meanwhile, are drawn like bees to sugar when they see Gabriel's sister. She has lush black eyes, polished skin, and extreme curves in her red suit. The way she holds her head—fierce and delicate—makes every guy in the room imagine doing what she tells him to.

Greg and his family make their appearance, his dad in pleated slacks and mandals with black socks, and his mom with Greg's almond eyes, both their lashes so thick the eyes look lined. The family smiles, moves confidently, but they're trying to resurrect an angry, ashamed, and disappointed son. Every time his mom touches him, he gets still as a rock.

"Philip, it was great catching up. Don't worry, we take good care of Laine." Dr. Ryan is finally breaking off a long chat with the Brecks—and a succinct introduction to the Olivettis. "Next time I'm in New York, I'll come by your office. We need to follow up the last Trustee meeting. I think you made some great observations."

Nikki is wondering if Mr. Breck's ass is sore.

"And Victor, it was nice meeting you and your family."

Laine and Nikki stand next to each other but avoid eye contact. Laine resorts to touching the swan's neck of an amaryllis stem on the side table.

Strangely enough, Victor and Philip are catching up like old teammates at a reunion. Victor is giving Philip a play-by-play from Friday's football game. Philip laughs sympathetically when he hears about the fumble. "Happens to the best. Christ, Victor, I had hands of stone."

Polly and Sharon haven't clicked. Polly's charcoal riding

suit, velvet headband, and Ferragamo flats go head to head with Sharon's fur boots, pink diamond earrings that drag down her ears, white jeans. Early on, Sharon tried to make nice with Polly, but after ten monosyllabic answers from her, she retreated into being the MILF in the room.

"So, Victor, we need to get you out on Round Hill one of these days. It's an old Walter Travis course. It's no Tillinghast, but it's a good track." Philip's genuine invitation catches Polly off guard and she coughs, midsip.

"Oh, excuse me. Went down the wrong pipe."

"Sounds great, Phil. And me and the boys could take you out on the boat. We got a nice Bertram 42, for deep water fishing. You ever go out on the inlet, go for some tuna?"

The ladies sense these invites are headed in the wrong direction and they're right.

Victor gets an idea, gestures at Phil as if his cup of tea was a glass of wine. "Over Thanksgiving, you guys should come out."

Before Polly or Sharon think of an "unfortunate" prior obligation, Philip replies, "Geez, that's a nice offer, Vic, but we'll be in London visiting my eldest son's family."

Polly's face softens when she realizes this excuse is actually true. She decides it's a safe time to chime in. "Yes, but we'd *love* to another time."

"What about Laine? Is she going with you? We'd love to

186

have her stay with us."

Nikki shoots her dad a look as if he just offered to murder a litter of kittens. She'd mentioned Laine was staying at school over break, but this is *vile* misuse of that information. *Taking her home would be like doing homework all break. This girl is so effing tedious, there's no way Plainview will tolerate her.*

"What a fine idea!" Philip says, in ignorant goodwill.

"Actually, that may work," Polly chimes in. "Laine's planning on staying on campus. Laine, honey, is that okay with you?"

Laine freezes up; her mother might sound like she's asking a question but she's actually in mother-daughter code, giving a command. Laine had sensed her mom's resentment when she turned down the London invite, *but this sure is a fucked-up way of getting back at me. I'm going to spend the weekend sucking on cheap tiramisu in a living room that's probably wired by the DEA or something, in a house guarded by stone lions. Charming.*

Laine scrambles. "Oh, wait, what about Dad? I thought I was staying with him?"

Her father goes on an elk-hunting trip over Thanksgiving, when he gets back from his annual Atlantic salmon fly-fishing trip on the Miramichi; he has every year since the divorce.

"Your father's going to be in New Mexico. Sweetie, you know that."

Laine likes that her mother leaves out the hunting part in fear of how the Olivettis might feel.

The silence hangs until Polly, who senses *God forbid* there might be a scene, speaks up: "Great. Laine would love to go."

Saturday brunch. The halls are flooded with perfume, the fragrance of expensive soap, dry-cleaning chemicals, pipe smoke. The parents jangle with charm bracelets, and heels click on the marble floors. No new student knew how territorial they'd feel until they were invaded. The urge to show ownership has resulted in kids doing a blasé strut, laughing grandly.

Other kids have games this afternoon, so Nikki takes her dad on a tour, flouncing, doing a Vanna White for him, showcasing the hockey rink as if it was a brand-new dishwasher. He walks with his hands in his pockets, the mild sun soaking his suit. He has a kid's smile.

"Nik, this is terrific. This is a good layout, I gotta think."

They pass an open athletic studio where two people of unknown gender fence.

"They look like beekeepers, right?" Nikki asks.

The only thing that throws her off is seeing Seth and Diego strolling in an overly deliberate way across the sixth hole, hats pulled down to their noses. She heard Chase talking earlier to someone about Seth being out of hand, hitting the chemicals. She strains to see his face, and senses that he's aware of her, but she resists waving.

In the music wing, they pass Jorgen and a girl playing cellos in a shadowy room, coffee cups on the carpet. They walk through the science building, with its sulphur smell and rainbow periodic tables. Vic's reluctant to step into any room; just peeking satisfies him. Nikki cajoles her dad, but he's adamant about not intruding, even when the room is empty.

"I don't want to disturb," he repeats.

Geese cross the sky when they walk to the main lawn. They both stand and watch. "Big trip ahead of 'em," Vic notes. "They're running a little late this year."

They pass a quartet of guys in Bermuda shorts, loafers, and fleeces playing paddle tennis on the raised, wired outdoor court. Vic asks Nikki what they're playing.

"Paddle tennis. You never played?" she kids him.

He grins. "At that age, I had graduated high school two years early, and was runnin' forklifts and chasing older girls."

The only place Nik can get him to sit is in the church. He relaxes in a pew. The windows are lavender, the old glass rippled. Light bathes the room in waves. The quiet makes an honorable, slow measurement of the day.

But they're there to talk. They both know it, and bask a few more minutes. Finally Vic looks at his daughter and the childishly charmed look is gone.

"The letter," he says.

"The letter," Nik repeats sadly, playing with the piping on the velvet seat.

They look at each other, and Nikki throws up her hands. "I mean, they would probably say the same thing to *you* if you showed up in a pair of black pants. But throw some whales or crabs on your slacks and you fit right in."

"You're gonna learn as you get older you got to *adapt* to succeed. You graduate and you go on to be a successful member of society, then you come back here, give a speech in your underwear, and they'll change the dress code in your honor."

"But, Daddy, this is *high school*. Everyone I know is having fun, and I'm getting lectured for wearing a miniskirt. It's just . . ."

"I know, honey, but you want to be better than these kids. I mean, that guy . . ."

"What guy?"

"Nicole. Come on, I'm not blind. The guy in the hat. Is he your boyfriend?"

"What if he is?"

"What's the story, princess?"

"What are you asking me?" she says with a hard edge.

He sighs, looks away.

Nikki glares at the stone floor. "Why do you never talk about the real stuff?" she hisses.

Vic is shocked. "What?"

"You know what I mean. We can talk about this letter and talk about my clothes. But we never talk about the real shit."

"What is there to talk about, Nicole?" her father asks sheepishly.

"*Everything.*"

Wellington wins against Kent. The Brecks see Laine—who started—score twice. A flick to the upper-right corner of the net, a drive through the goalie's legs—then they leave at half-time, waving, to dress for the Occidental Hospital Charity Ball that evening.

MK plays a total of twelve minutes, in the second half, when Wellington is leading by four. After the game, MK introduces her parents to most of the team as everyone mingles around the water bottles and towels on the bench. Laine thinks her mom looks kind, with a dark blond braid. Her dad wears a beige and mint tweed jacket with cream leather elbow patches, a sprig of yellow leaves in his lapel. Laine smoothes her hair as she approaches them.

But MK turns her parents away from Laine, and says loudly that it's late, and they need to get to the hotel because they have dinner reservations. The parents say good-bye to everyone, and move off.

13

The next Tuesday Laine gets her first one. She's talking to Nikki, in the antiseptically polite way they've developed—which has only gotten more formal since they were designated Thanksgiving buddies—and suddenly she feels a coldness in her nose. She turns and busies herself with papers, and sees a red dot on a page. Then another red dot. She grabs a tissue and pretends to blow her nose as she heads to the bathroom.

What is this about? Why are you doing this? But she doesn't know who she's addressing.

Winter in the woods is a new sound. Even the thinnest white layer will change voices, the way stories are told, the way they're heard. Crows caw more urgently. Plants persist in the lake, emerald in the cold murk. A canopy of black laces the ivory sky, Nikki stops and stares straight up.

"Okay, my friends," Grant says, clapping his gloves. "We're on the hunt for fallen branches, rotting logs. Let's find what mother forest doesn't want anymore."

They clear wood, pile it under a tarp. It will be used in faculty houses as firewood. At night, wood smoke will linger over the campus: a blue fragrance.

Sometimes when it's cold they cut the afternoon short, crowding into Grant's office as the sun goes down early and red. His papers are stacked under stones, pots hand-thrown in the kiln, holding pepperberry branches and feathers.

They look at maps and architectural designs for a new cabin Grant doodled, and talk about houses and shelter and what it means to make a home. He shows them a library book he discovered, a nature journal by a man who's been studying these very woods since he was a boy: a length of seventy years or more. It's his journal's pages that are reproduced here, pen drawings washed in watercolor and scratchy, block-lettered observations about chipmunks, ravens, deer, trees, leaves, fruit, raccoons. A fox.

"I know that fox," Grant says. "She is one classy lady. A loner."

"You see her?" Parker asks.

"Rarely. It's always a special day when I do."

In the past, if Nikki had been locked in a cell with this

book and nothing else, she would have gladly died of nervous boredom before opening it. But now she asks Grant to borrow it. The ink on the cardinal is so red she puts her finger to the paper to see if it's wet, knowing it is not.

Good girls never ride in the back of the bus, even in a top-of-the-line Starfleet Cruiser with cushy seats and flat-panel LCD screens. MK, Dana, and Kitty repeat song lyrics and movie lines, laughing and imitating voices from the back row, where they're crowded. Laine can't help but be attuned because their energy is riotous. MK's crew is loose, not the top players on the team, but saucy. Dana's ass is pretty grand, and she does impressions of Beyoncé talking to Jay-Z.

"It's your girl, Jigga. It's B. Where you at, baby?" She pouts, standing up to shove her booty in the aisle.

Their patois of inside jokes and references is not meant to exclude anyone, although that's its effect. *One* did *fly over the cuckoo's nest,* is one of their favorite dictums. The extended jokes they make and remake are constellations of detritus from academia, books, TV, highbrow and lowbrow films, hip-hop, country music, characters at school, philosophy, principles of physics. If it crossed their radar this month, it's been woven into the lexicon.

But closer to Loomis, Laine cranks "We Are the Champions" on her iPod. She *makes a movie.*

When they hit the field at first whistle, the weak wintry sun in everyone's eyes, Wellington feels good. MK is starting, and Laine's okay with that because it means MK might not give her dirty looks on the ride back. All the players have W's charcoaled onto their cheeks. Kilts rise above strong thighs as players tear the field.

The game goes awry when MK fouls in the circle. A penalty hit later, and Wellington is down 0–1. Miss H doesn't take her out, but then MK runs into an opponent in the end zone, and keeps striking after the whistle. This gets her a yellow card. Miss H is pushing Laine in as substitute when MK says something to the ref that no one else can hear but earns her a red card.

"Mary Katherine, get in here," Miss H says in her dangerous voice.

"I quit!" MK screams from the field. "I'm out. I'm done with this team."

Miss H sends Schuyler to get MK.

The bus ride back, *needless to say*, is quiet. Wellington won, 3–2, but that's secondary to the humiliation and chaos that MK has wrought. Dana and Kitty comfort her in the back row, and everyone can hear MK crying, mewing.

Laine sits alone, iPod jacked. Her shoulder's tapped. Schuyler's mouth moves. Laine takes out her headphones.

"*Great* game, Laine. Miss H told me this might lock you a spot on the All–New England team."

"Really?" Laine means: *Really, you can talk about this shit when this weird personal drama is going on back there?*

"So look, you have to—oh yeah," she says, pointing to the Jaeger LeCoultre watch, even though Laine wasn't looking at it. "Early Christmas, *beyond*, right? Can you believe I forgot to take it off before the game? *Hello,* there goes thirty grand. Close call! Anyway, you have to come to Heather's party in Darien over break. I'm getting flown in for it. It's going to be *epic.*"

"Can't. I'm going to Long Island."

"Strawng Island?"

Laine slowly nods, admitting defeat. "Yeah, to Nikki's."

"Umm. Excuse me. Do your parents not love you or something?"

"Let's just say it was a parent trap."

"Holy shit. You're going to Thanksgiving at the Sopranos. I think I saw that episode. Someone dies. You better watch out."

"Don't rub it in."

"Actually, this is perfect." Schuyler pauses. "I bet there's *priceless* pics laying all over her McMansion. You know, her cheesed up with Britney Spears hair, blingy bling and braces." Another pause. "Better *yet,* there's probably a few of her and her old Joey Buttafuco boyfriends, gym-heads with wife-beaters and man jewelry. You *have* to pocket a couple. Please? I know everyone would *love* to see Nikki during her head-gear years."

Laine knows that Schuyler will not leave her alone. "Sure. I'll see what I can find."

Schuyler squeezes Laine's shoulders and whispers: "You *do* know about Talliworth's letter home and how the whole faculty is talking about her, right? She's crashing, next comes burning. Cuh-razy."

For the rest of the ride, Laine replays the goals, her assists, the game, until the action whirs in her memory so fast the film should burn in the projector.

Laine wakes up two mornings later, and smells iron. On her pillow is a blossom of fresh red. She touches her nostril, looks worriedly to see if Nikki's awake, but she's not.

At the infirmary, she's rattled to see Chase, and rakes her white-blond hair with her fingers in a hurry. But he pats the wood bench, asking if she's there to get a sick slip from chapel.

"Um, yeah," she lies.

"Yeah, I'm going to get a slash if I don't have a slip for missing today."

Burns is there too, as he is most days. Chase tells Laine the Burns method. Burns sits there as though he can't hear, but he's blushing with pride.

"See, Burns here, every other night he goes online. Looks up his favorite illnesses, and learns new ones. Then he *combines* symptoms, and comes in here to give Nurse Sinclair a spiel."

Burns puts his head down.

"Last week, what was the trio, Burns, my friend? Autism was one, and Asian Bird Flu. And . . . I can't recall."

Burns grins. "Syphilis."

"Last year, apparently, he tried deafness. She kept asking what was wrong and such, and he was like, *I can't hear you.*"

Burns explains he'd just seen *It's All Gone Pete Tong.*

Laine smiles, having no idea who Pete Tong is or was, and can't help touching her lip to make sure there's no blood.

Nurse Sinclair plants herself in the threshold to the examining room now. A tattoo shows faintly under her white stockings. She reportedly sells Vicodin, but someone has to recommend you. Word is a senior named Wudtuth can broker a deal.

"Whatcha got, Burns?" she says. With big arms and hips, and rolls of strawberry-blond hair, she looks like a film noir killer.

Burns lifts his body from the bench. His blazer hangs off his bony shoulders like a coat thrown over a coat rack. "Nurse . . . ," he manages to get out before doubling over.

She remains standing, arms crossed. "What ails you, Burner?"

He looks her in the eyes. "In my lower, my lower abdomen, I feel these darts of *pain*, Nurse Sinclair. And I'm hot. And I feel like I've gotten bigger, like I'm holding water in my *flesh*."

Burns always uses Biblical words to hike up the drama.

But suddenly Nurse Sinclair looks alarmed that something is actually wrong. Everyone in the waiting room tunes in to the energy. She tells Burns this time he might be in serious jeopardy.

He perks up. "Really?"

She nods solemnly, wipes her palms on her skirt. "Burns, I believe you're about to menstruate."

The room snickers. The nurse sends Burns back to school. She beckons to Laine. "Do you have class first session? You're next."

After the nurse directs Laine onto the crisply papered table, Laine suddenly fears explaining. So she sticks to saying vague things about getting dizzy and feeling weak.

But as the nurse gets suspicious, Laine slows down the details.

"I got to ask you, honey. Do you think you might be pregnant?"

Laine laughs, unhappily, shakes her head.

"Because you do know that girls can get pregnant even if he pulls out at the last—"

"I know, I know."

"Because some girls think if you take a shower afterward, or if you use a feminine douche—"

"Well, I, uh, I'm not one of those girls." Laine smarts, feels like she's on the witness stand, her of all people—Laine Hunt, who's barely been kissed.

"Hmmm. Are you eating regularly? It's okay to tell me if you're not."

"I probably eat healthier than anyone here."

"Do you get your periods regularly?"

Laine got her period once at thirteen, and never again—which among serious athletes is normal, she knows. "Yeah, I do." She starts thinking fast. "You know what? I think I'm doing what my mother says I do, making a mountain out of a molehill. I can be a hypochondriac. And I should head because I'm about to be late."

"Are you *sure*?" Nurse Sinclair balls her meaty fists and anchors them on her waist. "Why don't you come back and see Dr. Littleton when he's in. Come back this afternoon."

"No problem, see you then," Laine lies. She knows a doctor will bar her from sports, not because he cares so much as he's got a healthy fear of lawsuits. Laine's also heard that Dr. Littleton believes colds, sprained ankles, and migraines originate in his patients' panties.

Laine can't look at Chase as she leaves. When she gets back to the dorm, Heather is leaving 407. Heather grins, displays a handful of Hard Candy makeup.

"We're just drawing a little chart of your friend, I'll return it all, don't worry."

When she sees Laine's surprise, Heather assures her it's cool. "Tradition, buddy! It's all good, Lainer."

Did she just wink at the end of all that? Can these people be so viciously corny?

The light dies early now, and everyone struggles against the shorter days. Nikki and Parker wait in flinty shadows behind the student center for the van to town, Parker in a nappy rabbit fur jacket and faded black jeans, Nikki tucked into a Diesel zip-up, hands stuffed in the pockets to keep warm.

Laine doesn't see them until it's too late to turn around. *Oh, come on, I just want to do errands.*

"Hey there," Nikki says. "You coming to town?"

Laine's hair glows in the twilight. "Uh, yeah. You?"

Luckily the van arrives, and Nikki and Parker pile into the back and Laine sits in the front. They drive through cool autumn roads to the village. As the van passes yards, the girls gaze at a domestic life they couldn't wait to desert, and now would embrace. Houses smear by—in this light the shingles could be white or baby blue or pale green, it's impossible to tell—windows burning gold, avocado pits in mugs growing tendrils onto kitchen windowsills, kids' bikes on lawns, plastic deer whose white spots shine at dusk, rose-bushes. When everyone steps out of the van, they smell the steam of early dinners in the air: garlic in butter, hamburger meat in oil, tomato sauce on the stovetop.

"Are you . . . coming to the supermarket?" Nikki asks, as Laine loiters outside the van.

"Gotta go to the dry cleaner's first," Laine lies.

As Parker and Nikki make their way into the supermarket, they look at each other. "I felt like I had to ask," Nikki says in her defense.

Nikki's never shopped for food before and Parker has to show her around. Nikki puts mustard in her basket, and Parker asks why. For sandwiches, she says. Parker explains that mustard gets refrigerated after it's opened.

"How do you know?" Nikki asks, reading the back.

Then they have a long discussion about bleach and detergent, Nikki's brow furrowed.

Afterward, they kill time at Maurice's Pizzeria, where they eat a slice, drink grape soda, and play pinball. Clumps of snow melt on the floor from the oven's heat. A local guy with a sparse mustache and tomato sauce on his apron tells Nikki to hit the ball right when it comes out of the machine.

She turns. "You want to take me on, my friend?"

When she laughs, he wipes his floury hands on his apron, takes up the challenge. They play a couple rounds, with Parker as the referee. Parker's actually involved, openly joking with a guy. *This is good. Gotta put training wheels on this girl.* Nikki makes Parker take over for her, and cheers them both on. The older guy behind the counter gives them a round of grape soda on the house.

They leave the dark, wooden place and walk in the cold evening. They wander to some picnic tables on the shore of the lake. It's so dark they sit there for a bit, smoking rolled cigarettes, talking in low voices, before seeing the kite surfers. Wet-suited people on surfboards harnessed to kites that capture so much wind the surfers fly. They sail above dark water, the wavelets pale and quiet, and crash into the water to let the wind lift them again. They drift from one beach of the lake to the other.

"Jesus, look at them. This is outstanding," Parker says.

Nikki nods in amazement.

Then Parker sees someone on the grass very near, the light so tricky they hadn't noticed. It's Laine, holding still to escape notice. She's been breathing the perfume of evening grass and lake air, luxuriating in not being at school and not being at home. A short respite from being any-where really. *Till now.*

Parker and Nikki stare at each other in the dark. Nikki murmurs: "Well, this is kind of uncomfortable." Then she says Laine's name out loud. "Is that you?"

Laine emerges from the darkness, carrying groceries. She earnestly pretends to be surprised. "Hi there, wow, you guys snuck up on me."

Nikki, who's opened her bag of Cheetos, offers one to Laine. Parker rolls her eyes in the dark. *I know. I'm like a scorned lover who keeps coming back for more.*

Laine actually eats a Cheeto, tries to smile.

The girls stand there, in the witching hour, blunder into small talk, then sit in silence. They're glad when the van rolls up because the threesome is too intense and strange. It's made them tired. They ride back to school in the dark vehicle without talking.

Nikki cruises past oak tables and ballpoint-carved wooden chairs, coat hooks burdened with Mount Gay Rum, hats and ski jackets bearing old lift tickets. The Susan R. Benson Memorial Library is bustling. Rows of new laptops are "occupied by students shooting off e-mails or IMing friends. Nikki hasn't turned on her IM account in months. LOOK-CANTTOUCH45 has been temporarily retired.

Nikki's meeting Seth in the viewing room, which has a lockable door and is such a hot spot there's a sign-up sheet at the library desk. Sessions in this room set fetishes; the only videos available are educational, so for the rest of their lives, men will cover their laps when they hear PBS opening credits. Women will get hard nipples hearing National Geographic music. Nikki and Seth like it in here, playing on the industrial carpet, black-and-white footage of the WPA flashing on their bodies, or kissing in green light from a science class video on algae.

Today she sprawls on the viewing-room floor, waiting.

They haven't seen each other in many days, at least not alone, and she's jonesing. The doorknob turns. He grabs her, holds her, kisses her.

"What's up?" she asks, pulling away finally.

But he doesn't want to talk. His face is intense and he pulls her back to him. A thrill shoots through her spine and down her thighs; she's never been held this way. They fall on their knees, he almost makes her lips bleed, biting, he holds her so tight.

They press against each other as if trying to become one person. Her shirt is off, her bra unlatched, she unzips him, they move fast. He's breathing harder than ever, and Nikki feels powerful for making him crazy. Before he takes off his pants, he pulls a Trojan from his pocket.

"Can we do this?" he asks, his voice is gruff, black hair hanging in his eyes.

She thinks about it for two seconds, maybe three.

Nikki always thought she knew what this would feel like. She's come so close to it enough times, it shouldn't be a surprise. But what is surprising to her now is how it feels extreme and it feels extraordinary but it feels more *anatomical* than *transcendental*. A guy's body is slamming inside hers. The bodies melt but not all the way, she doesn't lose her body into his.

At one point, she panics and almost throws him off, but regains herself and eventually starts to move, to buck. She recognizes her movements as what she'd been practicing through denim, in backseats of cars, in make-out sessions. All that heavy petting and experimenting was the body's rehearsal for sex.

"Jesus," he says now, his face ferocious. "Jesus."

Then he shudders, says *Jesus* again, but this time like a little boy.

His hot torso on her feels like ten times his weight, but instantly the sweat cools, and he withdraws, wincing. Stands up. Throws his garbage away. His face is red, his stomach mottled. He pulls up his jeans and boxers in one movement, stands looking down at the floor but not at Nikki. She feels cold and pulls up her panties, and her skirt down. She sits on the couch.

"Baby," she says finally.

But he's still standing in the middle of the room, staring at the floor. At first she assumes he's overwhelmed by how much he revealed, and how bad he'd wanted her. Then she worries she hadn't been good enough. Maybe he worries that she wasn't ready and feels guilty for pushing it. She should make him feel better.

"Baby, that was great," she says.

"I got expelled." Now he looks at her.

"What?"

"After the cabin, Talliworth told me there were two ways to handle our situation, but that I wasn't coming back after Thanksgiving."

Nikki stares at him. "What do you mean?"

Seth then holds up a finger. "One is to leave quietly." Seth raises another finger. "Or, two, they would send me to Disciplinary Committee, who would kick me out—and that would go on my record."

"I don't understand!"

Seth sighs, rakes his hand through his hair. His face is now pale, used. He shakes his head, looking at her, shakes it and wants to say something. "I know you don't."

And he leaves the room.

Dove-gray sky. Relentless afternoon, each minute lasting an hour. *I can't be out here.* Nikki looks with dead fatigue at the Suburban parked by a grove of naked birches. Her self, which she's trying to contain in her jacket, bleeds into the infinite woods, into the tangle of branches. She feels like she's gone missing, even though she knows where she is.

She asks Grant if she can go home. He says yes without pause and without asking why, and her eyes almost fill. His absolute answer is uncommon in this regulated world. She turns her back on the crew, who stop hammering to watch Nikki's breath roll over her own shoulder.

But she should have stayed. She's running back to her room too soon. She left before she felt the euphoria of being lost, which comes after the pain of being lost. She left before she came undone.

Later, after Check In but before Lights Off, girls lie in bed or brush teeth. Nikki's burrowed into her own bed, in pajamas, hands curled under her face as she tries to disappear. Laine works with just the desk lamp, trying to be quiet on the calculator.

No one knows what it is. No one's heard it before, except the older girls who promptly run through halls knocking on doors. *Fire alarm, get up and get out!* Schuyler actually tears off Nikki's comforter in a way that's meant to be playful but is not.

Outside in the cold, illicit hour, the girls can't help but preen. The air is strange, woods deeper, the wind alive. A fat moon plus a break in routine makes for pushing and shoving, catcalling and giggling. They stand in lines according to floor, in motorcycle boots and nightgowns and tweed coats, pom-pom hats and leather jackets and long johns. Frost makes the grass glitter like diamonds.

Heather had just applied a mint-green mask, and she walks from line to line, counting people.

"Okay, girls, up we go," the proctors say, herding their sheep once the fire alarm goes silent.

The second time it sounds, everyone is blasé and just moseys down the stairs. Heather's mask is half off. Schuyler announces that it's a malfunction but they're still required to bring girls out. Nostril hairs freeze as the girls breathe.

The *third* time, at quarter past midnight, Nikki stays in bed. Laine asks if she's coming and she says she is, but she's not. She listens to the building empty. *Good. Go away.*

Outside, Schuyler is excited Nikki hasn't come out. She tries to get Laine excited about it, asks if something's wrong. Then she tells Laine to get her. Mr. Lensk overhears, and in a rare moment of authority, tells Schuyler to go get Nikki herself.

Schuyler hangs like a big sister in the threshold of 407. "You have to come out."

Nikki doesn't answer.

"Hell-*o-o-o*! Get up, you have to come out. Fire drill."

"I just heard you say it was a malfunction," Nikki says without expression.

"It doesn't matter," Schuyler says with smugness.

"There's no fire!" Nikki yells at her, and seems suddenly tiny in the bed, her cheeks flush with anger.

Schuyler picks up Nikki's jacket with her pinkie. Holds it out. "Get. Up."

Nikki pushes past her, bumping her, this close to smashing her jaw.

Schuyler mimes astonishment. "Don't you want your jacket?"

"I don't want the fucking thing after you touched it."

Schuyler smirks after the bare-armed Nikki, and her

words take up the big silence in the empty dorm. "How mature."

Outside, there's quiet when Nikki joins the line, barefoot in the snow. Parker puts a lanky arm around her bare shoulders, sensing something very wrong, and rubs her skin.

Nikki tremblingly whispers to her: "*God*, any chance they get to fuck with me, they do."

"I know, sweetie," Parker says, awkwardly soothing.

"Jesus, I mean, what are we doing out here?"

"Fire alarm."

Nikki glares at her. "I mean, if Laine stayed up in the room, no one would have gotten her."

Parker smiles sweetly but sadly at her friend. "Is that a good thing? Think about it, love."

Nikki rubs her nose, looks at the ground. "This really isn't working for me, Park."

14

ad, hook up my iPod. I can't listen to Sinatra all the way home."

As they get closer and Nikki gets a rush of hometown vibes, she starts to dread the night's party. She's barely functioned since the viewing room last week (that's how she thinks of it, not as "losing her virginity," not as "getting her heart broken," but as "the viewing room"). Now she has Laine in Plainview. *How can I show up with this girl? People are going to think she's so stuck-up.*

Meanwhile, Laine stares at bleak Long Island strip malls and remembers Thanksgivings in Southampton with her cousins. Luncheons at The Meadow Club, Saturdays in Bridgehampton watching polo. Oyster stuffing and vintage champagne. *Jesus, why can't I be with them and not with Amy*

Fisher and Co?

The truck takes the Long Island Expressway exit for Plainview, and Laine sees people lined up outside the Olive Garden and Red Lobster. Wheaton Drive sits on the edge of Plainview, one in a line of white McMansions behind chain-link fences. They arrive at number 28 and for four days there will be no escape.

When they walk in, Sharon is kneeling on the white carpet and soaking up something with paper towels, bracelets jangling. "Ohmygod, he did it again, I let him in here for *one second*."

Vic throws his keys on the counter. "Where's my boy?" he asks, grinning.

Sharon sits back on her heels, red-faced but smiling. "Lainey, Nik, I'd hug you girls, but I got pee-pee on my hands," she apologizes, embarrassed.

Vic lets Rock into the room again, but Sharon doesn't protest. The Rottweiler puppy with the black and crystal collar comes swaggering, clumsily, up to Laine and bites her shoelaces. The elderly Madonna sniffs at Rock curiously—an old dame and a young boi. Vic explains they got Rock because their nest was too empty, and Laine looks up smiling, assuming he's made a joke, but his face is sad.

Thanksgiving dinner starts at four. Laine arrives in cream-yellow jodhpurs, a rust-colored cashmere sweater, and tall brown boots. "Jesus, Laine. We aren't going to the *stable* for dinner."

"Oh, Nikki. Laine looks absolutely gorgeous," Sharon says, herself in a black lace shirt, Seven jeans, and zebra Jimmy Choos.

Dolores bears a succulent turkey, carved.

"Il tacchino!" Vic exclaims.

Italian sausage stuffing, yams, green beans, cranberry sauce, mashed potatoes with Boursin creamed in, and a chalice of gravy get set on the dining-room table. The chandelier spangles the meal with rainbows, catching the last sun. Laine looks around the house, which is covered in white carpet. Lucite and white Formica is mixed with old wooden tables and religious hangings—stuff that belonged to another era, another country. It's amazing how a house can smell good, in theory, full of cooking and life, but when it's not your own, it smells horrid.

Laine notices Sharon swallowing her Ruffino Chianti, then drinks Tab. Vic also sips wine, trades looks with his wife. *Are they nervous about having me here? Is that possible? Is that what I sense?*

"Now, Laine," Vic says. "Don't be bashful. You work out so much, you should be eating for two."

"Uh, actually, just turkey and green beans will be fine for me. Thank you."

"You girls! Skinny as twigs. Dolores, load me up." Victor

says the most elaborate grace Laine has ever heard, and then they all lift their faces. "So, Laine." Victor forks together mashed potatoes, turkey, and, at his request, bacon. "Nicole told me all about your Championship games. That's real exciting."

"We're playing Taft for the New Eng—"

"Daddy, give me a bite of your potatoes." Nikki leans across the table, and he feeds her a fork of potatoes and cranberry.

"I'm sorry, Laine. You were saying?"

"I was just saying that yes, we play Taft next week for the New England Championship. The game's in Greenwich, though. It's played on a neutral site each year." Laine nibbles her turkey. Her plate is dissected: dark meat and skin to the side, beans and white meat in the center.

Nikki leans forward. "More, please."

Victor spoons her skin, bacon, cranberry sauce. Laine winces. Sharon's eyes glitter under mascara with pleasure and happiness.

I feel like I'm in some weird family foursome.

Dolores reappears holding two pies—apple and la zucca (pumpkin)—vanilla ice cream in an ornate glass bowl from Italy. She comes back out with espresso cups and orange twists on a tray, breathing heavily.

"Thank you, Dolores. *This* is what I been waiting for. Notice how I hold back this year, huh, gang?" Victor ridicules his three helpings, riling the girls up to eating mountains of pie.

When Laine declines, Sharon protests. "Laine, honey, your parents will think we starved you, the way you eat!"

"Don't worry, Laine never eats. She's a machine." Nikki lifts her arm and flexes.

"I am not!" And so Laine is guilted into eating a slice.

A Young Jeezy ringtone pings from Nikki's pocket.

"Oops. That's Ness. I got to grab this."

Victor winks at Laine as Nikki bolts upstairs. "What can we do, huh?"

After dinner they stand around the roaring fire with coffee, but since it's a global-warming weekend and 60 degrees outside, Vic blasts AC, too. On the mantle, pictures of Nikki in a cotton-candy-pink tutu, at Chuck E. Cheese in the ball bin, in a school photograph with white-streaks in her brown hair, and braces. With a woman in a bomber jacket and jeans on the top of the Empire State Building. With a steroid-jacked guy in formal wear, an orchid dying on her wrist. *Any one of these would be a great trophy for Schuyler.*

Nikki's taking her homecoming seriously, multitasking with hairbrush in one hand, lip gloss in the other, cell tucked under her chin.

"I'm hurrying, Ness. I'm waiting on Laine. Wait, I hear

her." Nikki pokes into the hall and sees Laine in workout clothes.

"Yo, girl. We got to get going, we got people to see and places to be."

The working out didn't cover the damage of that dinner, so Laine, with the shower running for noise camouflage, gets rid of it. She does this in extreme situations, and today qualifies. After showering, Laine pulls clothes from her L.L. Bean duffel. She throws on brown Levi cords, a Carhart jacket, and black Adidas Sambas.

And then she sits on the bed. Her body too depressed to even try to make it to Nikki's room. *I hate this.* Every threshold is gated, since the puppy pisses on everything. All day Ecuadorian guys who must work for Mr. Olivetti tramped through, laughing, talking loudly with Sharon in the kitchen. And this *room.* The closet is somehow wildly depressing just by being full of another family's objects: a plastic wrapped summer wardrobe, an old fax on the floor by a shoebox of vitamin bottles. It's gross. And in a glass vase by her bed is a red rose. *Like a bad hotel.*

She runs her hands through her hair and stands up. *Oh boy, here we go. Paint the suburban ghetto red.*

Nikki, focused in her mirror, looks to Laine's reflection as she walks into the bedroom. "You ready? Is that what you're wearing?"

"Yeah. Is that okay?"

It's okay if you hate yourself. "Yeah, whatever. I'll meet you downstairs in ten." Nikki's plan is dangerous: to lose herself in this life, this old life, and drag Laine along.

"This is fine Dad."

Mr. Olivetti pulls the Escalade under a streetlight two blocks from Plainview's Municipal Skate Park.

"Okay, sweetie. Now, you show Laine here a good time. You got that?"

"Of course." She kisses his cheek.

The girls jump out and walk to the park in silence. Bonfires roar in trash cans; kids huddle around cars in the concrete lot. You can't see faces, except in the few headlights shining on the half-pipe where skateboarders disobey a NO SKATING AFTER DARK sign.

Nikki gestures down the lot. "Ness said Mikey's Bronco is parked in front of the half-pipe. Let's make our way over there, cool?"

Each car shouts to Nikki like an old friend as they pass. Near a Jeep Cherokee, a black kid with a goatee and nose ring asks Nik where she's been and then flashes his new nipple piercing. As they pass a Honda Accord blaring Bloc Party, a wasted white girl asks Nikki if she wants a Jager Bomb. A Range Rover's tinted window slides down, and a smoky shadow asks if Nik wants "to get in on the hot-box."

This would be death row for Laine, but Nikki handles

the procession with verve. She speeds through each interaction, keeping them short but not rude. And then Laine realizes that *Nikki is liked here.*

A large group lounges around an orange Bronco II with its lights on. Nikki sneaks up and leaps onto a boy's back.

Still hanging, Nikki smiles. "Hey, people. You miss me?"

The group turns and Vanessa screams. "We been on the lookout for you. What the eff took you so long!" Tonight Ness is dressed one part Laguna Beach, one part Santa Cruz–hitting the SoCal skater chic even though she's never been west of her grandmother's in Jersey.

"Haven't you heard of fashionably late? Put me down, you dick!"

Nik drops down and gives Ness a quick kiss on the lips. She does the same for both boys.

"So, how's the new life, Nik?" one of the guys asks. "How's the peeps?"

"It's different." Nikki doesn't want to think about Wellington tonight. "Speaking of, I brought one of them home with me for Thanksgiving." Nikki turns and pulls Laine forward. "Everyone, meet Laine, my roommate. Laine, meet everyone."

Laine gives a little wave. *I want to die. I want to cut my neck with a rusty butter knife and die.*

"Oh shit. This is her?" Ness raises her eyebrows and acts

unimpressed. "Hey, Laine. I'm Ness. Nik's *best* friend." She turns back to Nikki. "Nik, Mikey's by the other keg. Let's go."

"Laine, I'll be right back." Ness and Nikki walk with arms locked, leaving Laine with two strangers.

Raphael and Craig drink Coors bottles and smoke blunts, their faces obscured by hoods. She can tell them apart only because one's a head taller–that is, until they speak.

"So, Laine. Whatcha do up there for fun?" the short one asks in a high-pitched voice.

Laine thinks. "I play field hockey."

"Field hockey, eh?" The tall one's voice could belong to a thirty-year-old. "I saw that once late night on a foreign channel. Except it was all dudes and they were wearing skirts. Pretty gay sport if you ask me."

"Dude, what the hell were you doing watching it, then?" The short one holds the blunt out to Laine.

Funny dig coming from two guys who obviously hang out with each other at all times. Laine uses a go-to. "Thanks, I can't. I've got a big game coming up."

The tall one sounds disappointed. "Shit, I thought prep school girls were all fucked up and wild."

"I think you got them mixed up with Catholic school girls." The short one laughs.

"Well, here, at least take one of these." The tall one hands Laine what looks like a wine cooler.

"Okay. Thanks." Laine reads the label: Jack Daniel's

Lynchburg Lemonade. *A poor man's Southside. This is shaping up to be one of the most astoundingly bad nights of my life.* In a way, Laine enjoys this, catalogs the absurdities. Even imagines reporting back to Schuyler after all, *because she will eat this stuff up.*

"Lookit, that kid DJing got some balloons." The tall one points over to a Mazda Miada circled by a pack of kids. "You want to suck one down?"

"No, thanks," Laine says. "I'm cool."

"I figured." The tall one continues, "Listen, when you get a little more corrupted and shit, come back and we'll party, okay?"

"You got it."

It's gotten cold enough to see your breath, but Mikey's wearing a mesh shirt tucked into cargo pants. His head shines.

"He's on fire. Don't you think?" Ness asks.

Even though she told herself not to, Nikki can't help but think of Seth: his untucked turtlenecks, plaid Brooks Brothers boxers. His bitten nails, the straight black hair covering one eye, the smell on his flannel jacket of cigarettes and trees and sky and *him.*

"Yeah, I guess." She smiles, not wanting to bum Ness out.

"Let's go talk to him."

Nikki's feet are made of iron, she can't lift them. "Shit. I feel bad about leaving Laine with those goons back there.

No telling what they've done with her."

"You don't want to check in on our boy Mike?" Ness is surprised.

Nikki pantomimes being burdened. "Yo, seriously," she says under her breath. "I got to handle Miss Connecticut over here. You go. I'll come back."

Laine is sitting against the Bronco's bumper, sipping her drink. *Not bad, but full of sugar.* In front of her, skateboarders are illuminated in the half-pipe.

She's watched X Games on ESPN but never seen this live. *Man, they're high.*

A kid drops into the pipe and slides up the other side. He turns, rockets down, glides up, turns at the lip, gains speed, and launches. In the air, he grabs his board while spinning his body, then lands like he's sliding across ice, smooth, and skates down the side of the ramp. Another skateboarder drops in and does the same thing. And then another.

How do they get enough momentum to get up the other lip?

One of them walks over to the Bronco. Laine watches him grab a beer from the cooler in the front seat, steam pouring off his body, crew cut soaked. The skateboarder sees Laine on the bumper. She's looking at him.

"You a new girl or something? Haven't seen you here." His voice more confident than the last two, but he looks the same age. He pulls a black down jacket through the Bronco's window.

"Nah. I'm just visiting. I'm with Nikki." Laine makes her unwelcoming face.

"Yeah. You look different. Nice jacket. What's your name?" He puts on his own jacket, covering the steam coming off his body, ignoring her hostility.

"I'm Laine."

"I'm Steve, Mikey's brother. You want a beer or something?"

"Sure," Laine says after a pause. Steve tosses Laine a Coors from the cooler. Laine opens the top.

"You been watching?"

"I have." *Great, he likes to be watched. The night gets better.*

"You see me fall? Oh my *God,* I took a digger. It was retarded."

"You did?"

"Holy *shit,* I ate cement. I ate it." He's laughing so hard it's contagious. "I had a TV dinner of cement. It was awesome."

"I guess I'm sorry I missed it."

Raises his pant leg to display the gash. "You know what it is? There is no *way* you can learn a trick without messing yourself up. So you can do the stuff you know how to do over and over again, right? And I know plenty of boys who pull that. Or you can bust your ass and try something."

Steam rises from his head. He swigs his beer now, thinking. Laine does the same.

He turns to her. "You want to skate?"

She laughs, husky but true. "Absolutely not."

"You been on a board before?"

Laine shakes her head, and he beckons for her to get up, thunks his board down on the pavement. Gestures to get on.

Laughing, Laine sets her beer on the hood, and steps up. He tells her how to move, demonstrating with his own shoes on the asphalt. She tries, and has to grab his jacket to stay on. He walks with her as she slowly rolls. She's laughing, and he grins.

"See? You're a natural."

Laine hits a bump and jumps off. Steve chases his board and flicks it up, throws it back down, and skates. He's circling her when Nikki comes back.

"What's up, Nik?"

"Hey, Stevie."

Nikki sounds resigned. "You wanna roll? Don't worry, I'm gonna take you home."

"It's cool," Laine says, too proud to say she wants to stay.

Steve yells out, as he does slow and elegant twists in the light, tells them not to go. "What is it, past you guys' bedtime? What the hell?"

Laine looks up at Nikki. "Won't Ness be pissed?"

"Nah, it's cool. She's got her hands full."

"You sure?"

Nikki is confused. "Yeah, I'm sure."

"Should we call your dad?"

"Already did. He's going to pick us up where he dropped us off."

Nikki and Laine walk away from the cars and the lights. "I'm sorry, I just feel like shit." Nikki looks sideways at Laine, then looks at the ground. "So, did those guys harass you or what?"

"Well, they asked me to do like ten different drugs, but that's pretty standard, I think."

Nikki agrees. "That's it? That's all that happened?"

"Well, I met Steve. He seems cool, I guess."

"Stevie? Did I tear you away there?" Nikki laughs. "I just thought he was fawning on you like every other guy you know."

"What are you talking about? No guy at school even knows I exist."

"Are you kidding me? What about Chase and his crew? They ask about you all the time."

Laine looks over at Nikki.

"Yeah, really. Do you think Chase is cute?" Nikki glances back, smiling.

"Well, I hadn't really thought about it."

"Well, we're going to have to think about this *much* much more."

They giggle. The Escalade is waiting, an almond-white moon reflected in its tinted window. The girls pile in. Victor is sleepy-eyed and wearing a velvet robe, hair slicked.

"Take us home, driver." Nikki plants a kiss on her dad's cheek as he pulls a U-turn.

15

Laine tries to sleep but she's restless. So she tiptoes through the Olivettis' hallway. A white-carpeted staircase spirals down, airstrip lights illuminating each step, and Laine thinks she'll just watch muted TV. *God, everything is so white.* This house is straight out of *Cribs*—just missing a dove-gray Bentley and an entourage smoking Thai blue and playing pool.

Nikki's door flashes. Laine makes out voices. *If she's just watching TV, will she mind if I knock?* She scratches on the door. Another scratch. Nothing. Laine pushes in like a cat burglar.

"Nik? You awake?" Laine whispers.

Nikki is fetal, cheeks blue in the light. Laine looks at the screen, and it takes a couple minutes to connect the dots. It's a training video, it seems, for forklift operators. A woman—earnestly and seductively, and with a thick Long

Island accent–explains how to use the machines. Her long nails trail the metal components as she recites her lines and then remembers to smile.

It's the bomber-jacket woman in the photograph on the mantle. And she looks exactly like Nicole. She must be Victor's sister, or a cousin. A close relation.

Laine has perched on the corner of the bed, entranced, and is startled when Nikki says, "Hey," in the dark.

"Hi, sorry, Nik. I couldn't sleep, I heard your TV."

Nikki, fumbling, sits up and rubs her eyes. She's slouching. Then she looks at Laine. "That's my mother."

Silence. "You look exactly like her," Laine says, unsure how to proceed.

"She died three years ago."

Laine looks back at the video. Her mouth literally hangs open. And she realizes what she's known all along—*this girl is motherless.*

Nikki laughs, but not pleasantly. "It's so retarded that I do this. My mom, she wanted to be, like, an actress when she was young. So she got this one job, this company hired her to make training videos. It was a huge thing at the time, for her, and it's how she met my dad, so I guess it turned out for the best."

"So you watch the tape sometimes?"

"No." Nikki snorts bitterly. "I watch the tape all the time."

Laine looks down to where her fingers are playing with the comforter. "I would definitely watch it, if I were you."

Nikki glares at her roommate, looking for sarcasm. "Are you serious?"

Laine nods.

Nikki looks away. Then at Laine again. "Want to go have a glass of wine?"

The girls pad down the hall, giggling and whispering, and pour glasses of red wine for themselves, sloppy, spilling. The fire has died to sleepy embers but Nikki rakes it, stacks more wood there. Laine looks at the photograph on the mantle, and realizes almost with surprise that she *had* been planning on taking it. She would have taken it, just because it was easier to appease Schuyler than confront her. Nothing happens to the fire, and they blow on it together. They wedge crumpled newspaper under the log, getting their fingers sooty. The paper smokes but doesn't catch.

"What the hell?" Nikki asks, but at that moment flames blossom, crackling.

The girls settle on the slate ledge, in their pajamas, holding their knees. They slurp out of the fat glasses. They share one of Sharon's Newport Kings, ashing into the fire, getting a minty buzz.

"So, you liked Stevie, huh. We could call him right now, you know."

"No!" Laine says, laughing raspily. "Are you crazy?"

"Yo, where did you get that laugh? I would spend *money* to laugh like that, for real. If a doctor could give me that."

"I'd make a good phone sex operator. Especially since that's, like, as far as I've ever gotten, whatever base *conversation* is."

"Wish I could say the same," Nikki says dryly, the first time she's referred to the viewing room out loud. It feels like a start.

But that's not what they discuss. Nor how much Nikki misses her real mother, how Missy smoked in that kitchen and counseled her friends on men, and made meatballs and fancy drinks, and combed Nikki's hair. They don't go over how Nikki used to do skits and recitals at her bedside, hoping to keep her entertained so she wouldn't leave them all. They don't talk about how Laine was also eleven when she parted ways with her dad. How if Nikki and Laine were records on a turntable, they'd have a scratch in the same place and a skip in the same chorus.

Nikki snaps her fingers. "I know."

Instead they make prank calls with Laine speaking lines that Nikki makes up, going through the directory of hot guys in Plainview, falling on the rug and laughing silently as guys try to get their bearings on the other line. The girls' teeth turn purple from the wine, and their stomachs hurt from laughing so hard. They eat the powdered donuts meant for breakfast.

Vic wakes Nikki the next morning, gently, standing in the threshold of her room with two cups of espresso, orange twists on the saucers.

"Can I come in, princess?"

She squints, rakes her hair back, and sits up. Nods.

They sip for a minute. Then Vic clears his throat.

"I'm going to tell you a story, Nik. Okay?"

"Yeaaahhh," she says uncertainly.

"First date. Missy—your mother—made me wait about forty-five minutes, talking to her dad." He coughs, a nervous tic. "But she comes down, *super*high heels, white, and this tiny dress with like a palm leaf thing, like a print on it. It's summertime, right? I was embarrassed to look at her in front of her father; I bet I blushed. She was beyond beautiful. *Bee-yond*. She wants to go dancing. We're heading into the city, for a big night out. My pocket stuffed with bills. We get into my Chevy Caprice, which promptly dies twenty minutes in, on the nice and sweltering Brooklyn-Queens Expressway."

He smiles sarcastically, shakes his head. "She makes us walk. Except I got to carry her half the way because she gets tired. We duck into some Irish pub, first thing we see. No one talks to us. She puts a mess of quarters in the jukebox. She's dancing. She gets this old guy to dance with her. Soon there's a *party* at Finnegan's or whatever it was called. She buys the bar round after round, on me of course. We listen to Whitesnake, Mötley Crüe, Guns N' Roses, whatever this stuff is. We listen to Irish ballads. We listen to Sinatra, "New York, New York."

"Luckily she gets the bartender to drive us home, lucky because I got *nothing* left for money, no cash for a taxi, no way home. She spent it all.

"Next day, it's *sizzling*, my buddy and me got the hood up on my Chevy on the side of the highway. And the heated up inside of the car smelled like her, her cigarettes, her shampoo. And I stopped working for a minute to remember how she looked on her parents' doorstep, shoes in her hand, blowing kisses to me and old Joey the bartender in his van, and she was laughing, for no reason, because the sun was rising, because she felt like laughing. And I knew I would marry her."

Nikki grins.

He finally claps her on the shin. "I'll tell you another story whenever you want. I'll tell you all the stories, kiddo." And he lumbers from the room, carrying their empty cups.

Lunch that afternoon is Italian style. Laine and Nikki feel shy and awkward, as if they hooked up the night before. Laine eats the lasagna because it's irresistible. In the background, Celine Dion and Josh Groban and Il Divo. Nikki rolls her eyes at Laine, explains that her dad learned to make mixes on his computer.

"What are you girls gonna do today?" Vic asks, his chair pushed from the table, his hands on his stomach.

"*You* choose," Nikki tells Laine. "We've been doing everything I want."

"Oh, God, I don't know. I'm happy to do whatever."

"What would you do if you were at home?" Vic asks.

Laine shrugs, smiles to be in the spotlight. "I guess riding. Horses, I mean."

"So let's go," Nikki says.

"Um, we need a horse."

"We'll find one online or something. Look in the Yellow Pages, Shar," Vic calls into the kitchen.

The Red Barn Stables in Oyster Bay is exactly that: a red barn. Geraldine runs the place, and is bossy, excited, and confident about getting Nikki and Sharon on horseback for the first time. She takes them by stalls and shows them picks for the ride. Nikki and Sharon wring their hands, look at each other, bite their lips. Finally Sharon interrupts.

"Ohmygod, I can't believe I'm such a coward, but I *cannot* do this. I'm too scared! Nik, you do it. I'm gonna watch you girls."

"Oh, come *on*, Shar," Nik says. "Do it! If I can do it, you can do it."

But Sharon stands, hands on her hips. Nikki takes a stocky gray quarter horse, and Laine gets a black gelding. Geraldine suits them in helmets and paddock boots. Nikki, when hoisted up, loses her breath.

"Holy shit," she keeps saying.

Geraldine lets Laine lead Nikki around the sand arena, and Nikki doesn't stop saying *Holy shit*. Laine is reminded of seeing her baby cousin put into a pool for the first time, and how his body bucked and shivered. Sharon sits in the barn's foyer in her Donna Karan hoodie, where a cat curls around a woodstove and poinsettias shiver. She holds a magazine in her lap but is smiling at her stepdaughter. When Nik gets off, to Sharon's applause, Nikki swears she's found her new thing.

"Did you really like it?" Laine says, leading horses by reins to the stable.

"Ohmygod," Nikki says, walking bowlegged. "I love it! I can't, like, walk because of, you know, but I totally *love* it."

On the way home, Sharon asks Nikki if she needs to get dropped off. "Yeah," Nikki says. "I'm early but that's fine."

"Where you going?" Laine asks.

"I just have to see someone, I'll be home soon."

Nikki slips into the room. They haven't seen each other in months, and the silence is long. She slumps in a chair, looks away.

Dr. Halliday has burnished cheeks, deeply carved lines in his face—a curved set fanning from his eyes. He looks like an aging Viking, with a blond and gray beard, darkly tanned and creased hands with impossible knuckles the size of gumballs.

"So, Nicole. What's the news? We have a lot to catch up on," he says, capable of stating things other people cannot pull off sincerely.

His ancient leather shoes squeal as he crosses the room with tea. He likes for them to have tea together, and today Nikki picks ginger. The black carpet is plush and strewn with kilims, their words gently absorbed.

"How are you? Let's start with you," Nikki says testify.

He sits in his chair. "Well, going through sailing withdrawal, since the summer. But I just went to South Carolina with my wife and we got our fill of sun and sail and water there."

Nikki's inwardness increases as she glares at the wall. "Your wife, I saw her name. She's on the Wellington board, she's the only woman."

"And I'm damn proud of her."

Nikki looks at him, eyes narrowed. "She pulled strings to get me in."

Halliday is speechless for a moment. "Why do you say that?"

"Because I don't belong. I knew it the day I got there. They never would have picked me if they'd had a choice."

Halliday squeezes the tea bag from the cup, lays it on the saucer. "Does it matter?"

"It sure does fucking matter."

"You deserve to be there," he assures her.

"Gee, thanks. That's an insult; the place bites." Her arms are crossed. She's looking at the wall again. Her face reddens as she speaks, "And I just decided the other day, I'm not going back. I don't have to take this shit."

Halliday sips his tea, waits.

"I came home, I didn't tell anyone my decision, but tonight I was going to explain to my dad. And I was not going to be convinced otherwise no matter what."

"And?"

She shrugs.

"Will you tell him?"

She shrugs again. "Things have changed."

"What kinds of things?"

"Too much to keep track of. I feel like I'm just, I dunno. I feel like I have to make it. I'm just holding on and making it through, and when the ride is over I'll be able to figure out what happened."

"Sometimes, Nicole, that's all you can do."

"You got my dad to tell me a story about my mom, didn't you?"

"I did."

"You mess around with my life."

"I do. It's incredibly unprofessional."

16

Schuyler grabs Laine the *minute* she walks back into Lancaster Four, pulls her into her room.

"So, what did you get at Nikki's house? Please say you brought me a little prezzie."

"No, I didn't actually. Never had the chance, sorry."

"Well, what were you doing the whole time?" Schuyler asks suspiciously.

"I don't know. Hanging out."

"That's it? You didn't meet any of her friends?"

"Yeah, I did. We went to a party."

"That must have been classic." Schuyler smiles. "Just *off the charts* cheesy?"

"Actually it wasn't that bad. Her friends aren't that bad."

Schuyler shakes her head. "Oh, come on. Give me the

real story."

Laine realizes she's shaking. "This tradition of yours . . . I don't know how to say it. It's *retarded*. So the school is hard for some people to get through. Big deal. Why do you need to make it harder?"

"Slow down there, Lainer, you're getting all crazy, it's freaking me out. You're going to have a stroke or something."

"Honestly, why are you doing this?"

Schuyler narrows her eyes. "What are you, on the PTA now? You're just a little black storm cloud, aren't you? I heard you think you're too good for everything, heard it before you even got here. I tried to make you part of things. But maybe you are just a *little too* snooty."

"It's not a tradition. It's hazing."

"Hazing? Are you accusing me of that? Ohmygod, conversation over. In fact, *relationship over.*"

Nikki wakes with a start, books in her bed and lamp on, even though it's 3 A.M. It takes a minute to locate herself. *Was there a noise outside? How did I fall asleep with books on my face?*

Oh yeah. It's index card time. It's footnote and bibliography season. It's Alderall and coffee and candy time. NyQuil to come down at night. Vivarin to get up in the morning. It's violet eye sockets and shirts on inside out time. It's time for Echinacea, Visine, cold showers. It's finals time.

Kids bump into pillars and chairs and other people, musty with sleeplessness. They huddle in corners of the library and dining hall and student center. Neckties loose. Tempers high. Nerves rough. In their sustained anxiety, people squabble about what X really does equal, and why.

Kids sleep a couple hours a night, nap erratically during the day. Walking through a dorm, one hears alarm clocks beeping, and it's obvious that someone in there asleep is too tired to even push snooze. The Upper-forms are zombies, since this term and the next determine college acceptance, which—according to many—determines destiny. It also proves to their parents that *we're worth it, we made good on your investment, we will become someone.* They can prove that living here, in rural Connecticut, has been justified, even though the family lives in Singapore or Minnesota or Colombia.

There's an informal ceiling, too, to how many from Wellington each college can accept. So students compete against their own friends to get into Harvard, MIT, Brown, Yale. At Wellington, the tradition thrives of posting letters—acceptances and rejections—on your door, and even months away, kids think now of what their doors will say.

During this week, sleep clouds waking life, and dreams breed.

At the moment, Parker's having a nightmare she's on a ship with Ben Franklin. *Parker,* he keeps saying, *tell me the name of this vessel, I know you know it, you learned it the other day*. And each time she peeks over the side, Ben comes up behind her and lifts her skirt, his white-stocking knees trembling, gold brocade on jacket glimmering, his face bearing a strange resemblance to Dean Talliworth, who teaches history. She's glad to be woken by an uproar.

Everyone in the dorm is crowding to the windows.

They can't tell who it is at first, but it's Chase sleepwalking in boxers and T-shirt and a cowboy hat someone left in his room. His bare feet melt footprints into the hoary grass. Ballast's been sent out by his wife, and he escorts Chase on his ramble, afraid to disturb him. They make an unusual, starlit pair—Ballast in bare ankles, pajamas, and loafers, and the open-eyed boy who can't see but walks in the dark.

Laine hasn't been studying right. Even Nikki asked yesterday if she was keeping up, which was one of their new-style exchanges: tentative and sincere. Laine keeps snapping out of reveries, replaying her conversation with Schuyler, adding things she wished she'd said. And her stomach is upset, she can't keep anything down. She's in this sour mood that afternoon, sitting at her desk, cold window open, sifting index cards, when Charlotte knocks.

"There's a man downstairs, in the common room."

"Who is it?"

Charlotte shrugs.

She pads downstairs to the TV room, opens the door, and is too surprised to hide it. "Dad!"

"What's up, sugar bear!" he says and hugs her, lifting her feet off the ground.

His body smells like tin, or minerals. He holds her away and they look at each other.

"Looking a little scruffy there, Pop." She giggles, already feeling giddy the way she does around him, even when she's trying to be stern.

"I'm going for that young Hollywood look. Whataya think?" He winks and does a spin with his hands out, sucking in his cheeks.

"Gotta lose the gut, first, Mr. Pitt."

Thomas straightens up. "You know what? Let's go to the Bluebell Diner, sweetie. I passed it on the way here. Let's have pancakes for dinner, like we used to do."

Laine rolls her eyes. "Dad, it's the middle of exams."

"'What's your name? Who's your daddy?'" he sings.

"You're such a dork," she groans, but has already capitulated.

The interior of the wood-paneled Wagoneer is dusty and sun-blanched, its floors covered with dead bumblebees and ginger ale cans. As they drive through Glendon, Laine can feel her dad appraising her, smiling.

"You're happy, kiddo?"

She gives him a look to indicate that of course she's happy.

On Sundays, years ago, Thomas used to go fishing with

Ben Talbot, and come home red from sun, smelling yeastily of beer. He would talk too loud, his gestures swung too wide, but he'd make the day's catch into a feast. Even their mom's silence—for leaving the family all day—collapsed as Thomas helped the girls chop herbs on a wood board, pour cornmeal, and slice the iridescent, tender fillets. Polly never let them help in the kitchen, or make a mess. Thomas reveled in both.

Sitting down to fresh fish and garden tomatoes, Thomas would ask his wife and daughters: *Are my girls happy?* Then they would eat ice-cream sandwiches outside, in the still hot though darkened garden, chocolate melting on their chins. He'd turn up Cat Stevens on their radio, and dance with his girls in the twilit yard.

And everyone *was* happy, until Thomas either quit or was fired—it's still top secret in the Hunt family—and started to spend *too much time* with Cat Stevens, with fish, with Ben Talbot, with Jack Daniel's.

"Here we go," he says now, opening the chrome diner's door.

Outside, potted azaleas stand brittle, frosty. Inside is the happy clanking of cheap spoons in mugs, the fog of sausage and coffee, the squeaking of the green pleather booth when they sit.

Thomas says it's good, no matter what, that she got out of Greenwich. It isn't the worst place in the world. "But it's a kind of Purgatory," he muses. "Lots of people with all the resources to be happy and none of the skills."

"Why don't *you* move then, Dad?" Laine says with just a touch of impatience. She's heard the Purgatory speech before.

"I might," he says, and makes his eyes twinkle for her. "Move up to the mountains, grow a beard, make friends with the coyotes."

"Seriously, Dad. Do it."

His eyes stop twinkling a bit. "I will."

"Live a little. Finally get that giant trout up at the lake, which I think is a *myth*, by the way."

He wipes his mouth with his napkin and then folds it and puts it on the empty plate. "Oh, the big trout," he says, looking for the waitress distractedly.

"Dad," she says, toying with the scraps on her plate.

"What is it, baby cakes?"

For some reason she tells him all about MK. She tells him silly things, like how MK wears a red coat that reminds her of Christine's coat, how MK's boyfriend, Toby, told friends he wants to marry her, that her brother holds three swimming records at UVA. And then explains how she's ousted MK, in her Senior year, from her position. Laine looks at her dad, having spread this all at his feet, and waits.

"Were you unsportsman-like?"

"No."

He shrugs. "Then don't think about it again."

"Is that it?"

He nods. "Do not get confused now, Laine. Be kind to her, and be honest. But don't compromise your, you know, *effort*."

"That was so easy," she says, half-joking.

"It's so interesting to me," he says, in his musing voice again. "Your generation, Laine, of girls, I mean. You got the go-ahead to compete any way you want. The freedom, you know, your mother never had. And you all took off, it's amazing. But you still don't know how to do it without feeling, you know, guilty."

"I guess," Laine says, unsure.

He looks at her seriously. "God, I miss you every single day."

She scratches her chin, uncomfortable feeling this happy.

When they walk out, the bell on the door jangles and Laine squints at her dad. Thomas takes the cellophane off his toothpick, and winks again at his firstborn daughter, and the cold late sun on his face makes him look radiant.

Nikki's finished her psych exam, after three hours in the gym listening to everyone carving essays into blue books. Her hand hurts, her mind stings, and her eyes are blurry. But that was her second-to-last exam, and she feels good.

She opens her mailbox. Inside a thin envelope is a letter that looks like the fiftieth time a schoolboy copied out the same message, and it pretty much is.

Nik. I've called and hung up. I've written this letter over and over. What it comes down to is I'm not good at expressing stuff like this, but I need to say something. So I will make it short, and I do apologize for the shitty letter-writing skills.

You are awesome. I miss everything about you. I hope what happened in the viewing room is not something you would undo if you could, because I wouldn't.

Seth

The bus catapults down the highway to Greenwich Academy. A few are carrying Wellington pennants, green W's on their cheeks.

"One thousand four hundred and forty minutes till we all get real fucked up. One thousand four hundred and forty minutes till we all get laid and do drugs."

Noah's rendition of "Seasons of Love" from *Rent* deafens everyone on the bus. Gabriel, Chase, and Greg pretend not to know him; they've learned that Noah infuriates upper-classmen, without even trying. Noah's gone face-down in a toilet heaving up some Senior's tobacco spit more than once, and was tied naked to a Glendon flagpole with a sign: THE REVOLUTION IS OVER. CUT YOUR HAIR AND SHAVE YOUR BUSH. He was picked up by cops before anyone could harm him. He never opened his mouth to say who was behind it, which helped him to live it down but did not quite extinguish the shame.

"Yo, Park! You gonna join the revelry in NYC this weekend?" Greg throws his forearms across Parker's chest to give her a hug from behind. "Leave your goddamn still life for a minute and go party?"

"I am. Staying at Noah's with all of you. Fancy, right?"

"This is going to get messy, my friends," Chase says. "What's the deal, anyway, y'all? Gabriel and I are riding down that afternoon." He looks over at Greg and smiles, speaks in his Biggie Smalls voice: "In the E Class, *nigga*."

"Your country ass don't know shit about the E Class, white boy." Greg laughs, half kidding.

Noah waves the group in tighter. "My parents are heading out to the Museum of Natural History benefit at eight, so roll over any time after that. I already got my brother picking up booze and some other shit."

"What else are you thinking?" Nikki inquires.

"I don't care—'shrooms, blow, X, bud. You all tell me," he brags.

"Definitely get some bud for me and Gabe," Chase says. "He's been pulling on my one-hitter lately when I fall asleep, and I'm running low."

Everyone except for Chase peers over at Gabriel and laughs. He was the remaining sober friend. Guess not.

"G-man, 'bout damn time." Greg gives him a pound. Gabriel blushes.

"Actually, I'll just tell him to grab what he can. We can give it out at Schuyler's party if we don't want it."

"Are we really going to Schuyler's?" Greg asks.

Chase nods. "She wants me. I can tell. We've been clicking like a couple of summer crickets lately." He's joking, but not completely wrong.

"All right boys, we'll drink and see if you all don't puke." Nikki sticks out her tongue as the bus pulls up to Greenwich Academy.

"*One thousand four hundred and forty . . .*"

"Honestly, Noah. Shut the fuck up." Chase and Greg slap Noah on the back as they slush through muddy left-over snow.

The fields are manicured to the *blade*. Normally, the groundskeeper wouldn't allow tailgating, but the New England Championship is the last game—plus the all-girl academy's $300 million endowment makes grass grow back faster.

Tailgating here doesn't mean bratwurst and Budweiser; it's duck paté, bleu cheese and walnuts, martinis in thermoses. White linen and silver adorn card tables set up beside cars. Leashed onto each SUV is a spaniel, setter, terrier, or retriever. The hunting dogs and Barbour jackets indicate a foxhunt more than a sports game.

"I usually like dogs, but . . . ," Chase says under his breath as they pass a snarling King Charles.

The Tods loafer–wearing owner apologizes. "Excuse Bunnie. She's not used to this much excitement."

"It's okay, neither is Chase," Greg says.

The man doesn't hear, pulls the leash, and wipes his forehead with a plaid Burberry handkerchief. "Naughty girl, now, Bunnie-bun. *Please* behave."

During warm-ups, Laine sees faces on the sidelines; her old coach and teammates from Greenwich Academy, former dance partners from the Brunswick School, family friends from Round Hill, coaches from camps, and Parker, Nikki, Gabriel, Greg–and Chase. Her parents are in Tokyo, and she had hoped the Millers would bring Mags and Chris, but she doesn't see her sisters anywhere.

As she stretches on grass apart from the others, Laine watches her movie: She's running crisp, passing clean, shooting hard. Schuyler hasn't looked at her once since their exchange. Laine feels alone on the team. Heather, though, is heading over now.

"Hey," Laine says nervously.

"Hiya!" Heather sits down to stretch. "So I just want to tell you, *big mistake* with that hazing accusation. Big, big mistake."

Laine starts to explain, but Miss H is calling the players into a huddle.

Heather whispers to her. "Hazing comes right after date rape. It's *not* what you accuse your proctor of doing. Did you tell anyone?"

"No, I–"

"You better not have."

The whistle blows and the first half is underway. Laine scores early during a man-up situation, but Taft ties. Normally, this is when Laine switches into higher gear, but today the close ball seems farther away, her cuts not sharp, her passes not crisp. When she tells herself to go faster, her legs won't listen. And the harder she concentrates, the more disconnected she is from her limbs. She's a ghost of her own body, trying to catch up.

What the hell is wrong?

At halftime, the score is 2–1. Taft is up. Miss Hartford pulls Laine aside in the locker room. "What's going on, Laine? You don't look like yourself out there."

"I'm fine, I just need to focus. I'm sorry, Miss H."

"I worry when I see you *dragging*. Did you eat right today?" Laine thinks she can hear exasperation.

"I did, I did. I had a potato and a bar, some cranberry juice. I'm stocked." *Battle your way back into the zone. Do whatever. It is impossible to fail today, or even to falter.*

"You didn't party over Thanksgiving?"

"No, I really didn't."

"Do you feel like you can start second half?" Miss Hartford is tapping her clipboard. "Dick Jameson from Dartmouth is here. I want him to get a good look, but not if you don't feel like you'll make the right impression. I've spoken about you, and I don't want to look like a liar. Think about this, Laine." Miss H laughs to lighten the statement, but it comes out thin, bitter.

"I'm fine." Laine shakes her head. "I just have to get going."

She hands Laine a water bottle. "Here. Drink. If you eat now, you'll get cramps. Let's go. Pull it together. If you go in now, you must keep it together, that's the deal here, player."

Laine pulls on the water bottle. She feels better. *Okay. Shake it off. I can do this.*

Miss Hartford's half-time pep scream shows dividends early when Heather scores to tie. But their momentum doesn't last long, and Taft is able to control the ball on offense most of the second half. Taft scores two goals to go ahead 4–2.

It's obvious that today Taft is the better team. Laine knows there won't be many chances to even the score, so on a long defensive clear, she sprints with everything in her. *Yeah, this is fifth gear. Runcrisp. Runcrisp.*

But as Laine nears the ball, a Taft defender swoops in to

whack it out of bounds. Laine exhales and slows to a jog. Then to a walk. She feels like a spent wind-up toy, power-less. She bends over, placing her hands on her knees. She gags. Nothing. Her legs twitch and her breath echoes in her ear canals. Everything else has gone mute. She can't hear Miss Hartford yelling from the sidelines. She has to lie down.

The first person above her when she comes to is Pug. Laine sees his lips move but can only hear her own breath. Pug hands her a water bottle and motions to drink. Laine sits up. She sips. The shaking slows and she can hear voic-es around her. Pug asks if she's okay. Laine nods. Pug and his assistant lift her off the ground and Laine puts an arm around Pug for support. He tells her everything will be fine. Laine looks back at Miss Hartford on the sidelines—her stare is intense. They walk slowly off the field into the lock-er room.

"Lay back on the table, Laine," Pug says as he sets up an IV. "This is just gonna feel like a little prick, but afterward, I promise, you'll be feeling good as new."

Laine lies back on the trainer's table. She feels the pinch and then some heat in her arm as Pug slides in the tube. She closes her eyes.

When she wakes, the room is dark. She has a visceral memory of coming out of recovery from a horse-riding fall when she eight. She woke on Christmas Eve. Everyone thought she should stay home from caroling but she threw a tantrum. That night, Polly held Laine's hand tightly, and Laine sees now her hand in her mother's, the fur cuff, candles lighting the night as they moved from snow-dusted house to house, singing. It had seemed that the lights were for Laine, that they had been lit because she woke up.

Laine is already in bed. Nikki, just getting back from dinner, looks at her roommate, sees the IV's bruise. Laine is pale, closed. Miss H never came by to see how she was doing. Neither did Schuyler, her proctor, her captain. Laine knows all she needs to know.

"You okay?" Nikki asks.

"Yeah." Laine stares at the wall.

"You want to talk?"

"Not really."

"For what it's worth, I think you played so well. You ran out of gas, that's all."

"Thanks."

Nikki tiptoes, changing, shutting off lights. They're both in their beds, no noise, and Laine feels it coming. She tries to tamp it down, but it's relentless. She runs to the bathroom.

And she starts to cry. Weird, humiliating whimpers. Terrified someone will hear, she strips and gets in the shower, turns the water on full blast. She didn't bring a towel and doesn't know what she'll do when she gets out but she bawls now. She cries so hard, water running down her face and body, that she has to sit down, her skin on the dirty tile. Each time the shudders slow, she bawls harder, head aching.

Laine hasn't cried in four years.

"

17

"Yeah, we'd like a bottle of Patron and Grey Goose. You can just throw it in the limo." Noah fiddles with his Armani tie and vest while talking on the kitchen phone. He decided against traditional bow and cummerbund after seeing Jude Law take the alternative route in *Esquire*. "Yeah, it's waiting outside. We'll be down in a bit. Yeah, just put it on my dad's account. Merci, Jean-Luc."

One West 67th Street is well known for its Gothic architecture and storied liberal past. Avant-garde painters and modern dancers used to call it home, but NYC real estate has long since priced them out, and the Park Avenue crowd has moved in. The famous and very expensive restaurant located in the building, Café des Artistes, raised its prices to reflect this shift, but also managed to retain some of its joie de vivre; a perk for the degenerate rich kids now living upstairs.

Noah's apartment is a sprawling duplex with floor-to-ceiling windows overlooking the Central Park meadows. Tonight, though, no one cares much about the dramatic view—it sparkles and twinkles in the background, and they appreciate it peripherally. Noah's parents are at their benefit, and the Wellington Lower-forms are focused on the task at hand—catching a buzz. Even if the Michonnes were home, the space is so big they wouldn't hear the kids partying, no matter how drunk they got. But the fact that they'll be home eventually was a bargaining chip in getting certain parents' permission for their daughters to stay the night.

Noah hangs up and turns to the crew hovering around the kitchen's marble-topped island. Crystal glasses crowd the middle of the counter and Bud Light cans scatter the perimeter. Robo-pound is on hold.

"Well, that should cover us for the ride to the after party. Whose turn is it?" Noah rubs his hands. "Laine, come on, get in on the action."

Laine is sitting on a stool a few feet away.

She smiles and lifts her beer. "I'm good."

"Come on, Laine, you've been nursing that beer for like an hour."

"I'm pacing myself tonight." Laine smiles apologetically. No one can argue after what happened on the field just two days ago.

Nikki raises her half-filled glass. "Here's to pacing." She taps Laine's beer.

The rest aren't concerned with moderation. Their pre-game prep for the Gold and Silver Ball has consisted of bouncing quarters, pounding Bud Lights, and taking bat hits.

"Dude, kind vids with the booze." Chase pays Noah a boarding school compliment. He's holding a quarter between his thumb and index finger, leaning against the island. Nikki thinks he looks straight out of a classic movie in his father's tux. Earlier, Chase found a forty-year-old coat check ticket from some cotillion in Georgia in the pocket.

"Noah, don't they care that you're underage?" Parker's wearing a frothy white vintage dress, and Nikki has done cat eyes on her. She looks beautiful, in her lost-in-time way.

"It helps having a running tab at a restaurant like Café des Artistes in your lobby. I've known the host, Jean-Luc, for years. He's a total pompous ass but he doesn't give a fuck about American laws." He looks in Chase and Gabriel's direction. "Plus, if either of you tools doesn't get any action tonight, you can pick up one of the high-class hookers who troll the bar."

Chase grins at Gabriel, who's barely tall enough to shoot quarters on the counter. Gabriel has his jacket off and his cummerbund rides awkwardly up his stomach. He reaches into his pants pocket and pulls out his wallet. He looks inside. "We're good."

Chase gives a fist pump.

"You guys are sick." Nikki smiles.

The group laughs. Tonight has promise. Bracing for the rest of the world they know they'll encounter later has consolidated this motley gang. Laine felt it when she walked into the apartment, after getting dressed at her aunt's place. And she could see surprise in everyone's eyes at how she looked. No one knew what to do. Could you tell Laine Hunt she looked beautiful?

Nikki had taken over and purred: "You look *dreamy*, my dear."

Everyone's adopted adult language, the formal, heavily perfumed affectations of partygoers, and they are pulling off this performance of maturity—until Noah farts from all the Chinese food he just scarfed, and Chase and Greg mock-box until Chase almost backs into the Julian Schnabel painting, which makes Noah bug out. Nikki keeps pulling up Parker's skirt.

"I'm sorry!" she says. "It's just so fluffy, I can't help it."

And Laine kind of *does* feel dreamy in the green velvet dress. The gown has more dimensions than seems possible; it has metaphysical folds. Where she's lean, it's voluptuous. Where she's shy, it's brave. Somewhere along the road in her life, she'd designated green velvet as a rite of passage. Maybe it was from a tale of her grandmother's life in Stockholm, or from a storybook.

She'd bought it the Sunday evening Mr. Olivetti drove them back to school after Thanksgiving, and they stopped in Manhasset to get Nikki a dress. Nikki didn't find one, but when Laine saw this dress at Carolina Herrera, which was about to close, and Nikki saw her looking, she made her try it on. Nikki was speechless in that mirrored room. She demanded Laine buy it, and when Laine explained she had no money, Nikki threw it on her AmEx.

"This is an emergency, my dear; you can pay me back whenever."

Walking through a windy, wintry parking lot to Vic's truck, Laine had held her garment bag and looked sideways at her roommate. *I can't believe I got it.*

They start them young on the charity ball circuit in NYC— not that the kids going give a shit about the endangered species or third-world countries they're contributing ticket money to save. The Goddard Gaieties at the Plaza is the first chance for seventh- and eighth-graders from all-boys schools like Buckley and St. Bernard's to get hard-ons in tuxedos while slow dancing with more developed girls from Spence and Chapin. And the Holiday Dance at the Waldorf is the prime opportunity for ninth-graders from schools like Collegiate and Nightingale to hone their rum-running skills.

But the Gold and Silver Ball for tenth- through twelfth-graders is an annual Prep School vs. New York City Private School All-Star game.

This year, the Ball's at Fizz on East 55th. A fleet of limos and a snaking line of kids in overcoats and furs wait outside. Big snowflakes swirl in the New York City night. A gigantic older black man in a long leather coat stands behind a velvet rope. The Wellington gang finish off their Patron and climb out of the limousine.

"Shit, look at that line. We're going to freeze our asses off out there." Nikki's black strapless dress is practically see-through tonight.

"I know the guy at the door. Follow me." Noah waves his posse on, and they all feel the stares of kids waiting. A couple girls shout to Noah, but he waves them off. "I'll see you in there." He's in his element. The only thing missing is paparazzi. Oh wait, the camera crew is flashing inside.

Inside Fizz, it doesn't take long for cliques from different prep schools to stand out. The long-haired St. Paul's eccentrics lurk behind sixty-foot-tall velvet curtains and sneak hits off computer dusters stuffed in their pockets. The wasted puck-heads from Avon Old Farms are already getting thrown out for fighting with rivals from Northfield Mount Hermon. The NYC girls from Chapin, now at

Deerfield, are grinding with their old Knickerbocker Dancing School partners from Buckley, who are now at Hotchkiss. The jaw-gnashing Taft crowd is getting interrogated about who threw up on one of the indoor plants by a pointy-nosed gray-haired chaperone. Seniors from Andover and Groton, who weren't invited to any of the cooler parties elsewhere, are huddled by the dry bar, pretending they aren't interested in the predominantly younger crowd.

Nikki keeps seeing Seth, upstairs on the balcony with a girl in turquoise spangles, or on the men's room line taking fast tokes off a roach with a friend. But it's never him, just sadly made fakes. She knows she'll see him tonight; he promised to be here or at Schuyler's, and besides, she's too high on the energy of the night to be broken yet. Her own high party point, before this, was prom as a freshman with Jason Turrino, decked in white Versace that her stepmom's friend finagled in the garment district, drinking Cristal—even though "prom" hadn't amounted to more than a group hand-job-a-thon in the crowded back of a stretch Hum V. She broke a nail that night and got an AIDS test the next morning. *You can never be too careful.*

Now she likes how her Wellington crew stacks up against the competition. *A cute Southern boy. A foreign politician's son. A New York City bad boy. A bohemian. Even Laine, in that green velvet, looks famous tonight.* So when Patrick

259

McMullan asks Nikki to stand next to Noah for a picture, she feels like a star. That is, until the gang from Holderness roll in like criminals from *Reservoir Dogs*.

"Shit, who are those guys?" Parker asks Noah.

"Oh, I used to know the guy in the middle from Saint David's," Noah explains. "He's a real fuckup. He got kicked out of Taft for videotaping a chick giving him head, and St. George's for selling acid, and now he's at Holderness—limited time only, most likely. If you want some nice bud or X, they're the ones to talk to."

"Good to know." Chase smirks. "All right, who wants to shake it up? Laine, let me show you how the Southern boys do it." Chase grabs Laine's hand and pulls her toward the dance floor. Laine feigns resistance but gives in quickly.

She feels brave tonight in a way she hasn't felt in many years. *I mean, the semester's over. I did it. It's done.* She laughs, stepping back and forth awkwardly, since she never wears heels, and laughing as Chase works overtime to amuse her.

And that's the Gold and Silver. A hustle of metallic dresses and velvet tuxedo slippers and cameras flashing and kids gossiping and girls putting on lipstick in the bathroom after puking and guys slipping pills to one another when no one's looking. The Ball itself is just a hinge for the partying that comes before, and, most important, the partying that comes after. Once the buzzes wear down on the dance floor, crews re-form and move on.

The 60 Thompson hotel is nestled in West SoHo on a quiet block of boutiques and restaurants. Pine wreaths hang in the heat-lamped outdoor lounge, and hipsters, models, rock stars, and businesspeople slouch in the downstairs bar waiting to be seated at Kittichai. Schuyler's father, Dick, arranged the celebrity suite for his daughter for the weekend and has gone out of his way to ensure that 60 Thompson's private roof deck, A60, is reserved for his daughter and her friends.

The crew gets in the elevator after passing through the über-chic lobby and giggling in the bright lights. Snow on their coats, pints in jeweled handbags, joints in the inner pockets of their tuxes—they're locked and loaded.

Upstairs, Chase swings open the door to Penthouse B with Laine, Nikki, Greg, Gabriel, Parker, and Noah behind him. Kids mill around the space. One yells, "Looks like the Gold and Silver kids have arrived." More catcalls ring out from the crowd of thirty or so: "Nice fucking tux!" "Who brought OJ?"

Laine is immediately uncomfortable and can sense her whole group feels awkward, pulling even tighter together. *We've gone from barely being friends to being a bona fide clique tonight.* This isn't just Wellington kids, as they'd expected. Not at all. These kids are mainly older, and from private city schools and boarding school rivals. The guys wear vin-

tage corduroy jackets, T-shirts, Salt jeans. Carbon copies of
Sienna Miller sport bangle necklaces and bracelets, cashmere scarves wrapped around Yellow Fever tank tops. The
air is thick with pot smoke. The walls are paneled with
leather. The world shines and flashes beyond the huge windows.

Schuyler waves the crew in, only making eye contact
with the guys. "Come on in, you freaks. Welcome to Chez
Schuyler. Booze is over there, help yourself to drinks."

"Nice, thanks," Chase says, as their ambassador.

Schuyler makes a curtsy in her orange dress. "Couture
Valentino, *hello*."

So the group moves en masse to the kitchenette, where
Stoli Gold sits next to PBR, Johnny Blue next to a crystal
glass of dip spit. Lemons on the floor. Cigarette butts in the
sink. Noah pours drinks, and they all start to loosen up.
Nikki feels a lightness, a suspension of gravity–the Senior
girls that so often pin her to the wall are otherwise occupied. She doesn't quite know that's the reason, but she feels
free.

They all toast one another, *cheers to their crew.*

"Well, we made it," Chase says.

And each one feels lucky.

They branch out, Parker taking bat hits with a hippie
from Deerfield, Noah setting up speed quarters on the glass
coffee table. Nikki looks for Seth, praying he's behind one

of the doors. Someone points to the back room. She pulls Chase with her.

"Eh, C-bass! Come in, my friend." Diego is sitting Indian-style on a king-sized bed still crisp with Frette sheets. The headboard is made of dark, glossy wood. A mirror lies on the sheet.

"How's it, D?" Chase drawls, ice clinking as he drinks.

Diego divides white lines with his Wellington ID. Orange stains the bottom edge from crushing and cutting Adderall all semester. "I gotta tell you, my friend. I'm pretty content at the moment. How 'bout yourselves? Can I help you to be any more content? Some Bolivian Marching Powder?" Diego peers over to Chase.

"According to Bret Easton Ellis it's 'the devil's dandruff,'" Chase says. "But I'm good."

"Only in fucking boarding school would we quote two authors in reference to cocaine. It's a lovely stupid country, mates." Diego inserts a tightly rolled hundie and vacuums two lines. He leans his head back and sighs. With a moist index finger he rubs remnants over his gums.

"Um," Nikki says. "Is Seth coming?"

Diego shakes his head. "Sorry. His dad's got him locked up."

Nikki sighs bitterly, absorbing. "What a dick."

"His dad?"

"No, Seth!"

"Easy, now, sister. After all, it was your cigarette that got him booted."

Nikki's jaw drops. "Are you serious?"

Diego looks up from his work, realizes she didn't know. He pulls white clumps from his nostril. "Babe. I'm sorry. That's not exactly what happened."

Nikki looks like she might cry. "Holy shit . . ."

"Honestly, Nik. Let me tell you something. Seth was never going to make it through that place. He lasted longer than anyone thought, and it was partly you that kept him there. So *scratch* what I just told you. You'll see him again."

"Really?" Nik says hopefully.

"I would not lie. He's my boy."

At the bar in the main room, Schuyler finally approaches Laine, who's nervously downed a glass of champagne waiting to see how Schuyler will treat her tonight—*I shouldn't care, but damn, it would be nice to close out the year without bridges burned*. Schuyler, barefoot and more flamboyant than usual, calms down as she takes the stool next to Laine. She licks her lips as though nervous.

"Laine. I got to tell you. I screwed up."

Laine's heart rate doubles. "What do you mean?"

"Not just with the bet, but with you. You stood up for your roommate and that's, I mean, that's the real shit, babe. That's what we're here to do. Do you know what I'm saying?"

Laine nods, hiccups Veuve Clicquot. "I do, Schuyler. I'm just sorry, I mean, I'm sure I said things too that—"

"Hush." Schuyler smiles, tucks her tawny hair behind her ear to display walnut-sized diamond studs. "God, I'm glad that's behind us. That just sucked, being at odds with each other and stuff. By the way, is that Carolina Herrera? It is beyond gorgeous."

"Thank you," Laine says, her eyes somehow mysteriously welling up with appreciation, and she hiccups again, laughs. "Whoa! Not used to champagne, I guess."

"Bubbles are good for you, Lainer!" Schuyler rubs her belly. She suddenly sits up, seemingly struck by a great idea. "I know, why don't we toast each other."

Laine thinks of saying no since she's already unsteady, but this is important. Schuyler pours two flutes, and they clink and sip.

"So, no one crashed?" Laine asks, feeling bold.

"I guess it wasn't meant to be, right?" As Schuyler's saying this she's waving Heather over. "It actually makes me feel better about the whole thing. I know! Let's toast to that!"

Schuyler pours shots of 151 Bacardi into the now empty glasses, and Heather joins them. Or rather seems to, as neither Schuyler nor Heather drink theirs. Laine doesn't notice, and has trouble getting hers down.

"Come on, you superstar. No sipping."

Laine tries to follow their conversation, although it's getting difficult. Schuyler and Heather laugh about leaving the boys in line as they crossed into Bungalow 8 earlier.

"You should have seen Diego's face when Armine told him no. I love that he pulled the 'Don't you know who I am?' card. That place is so fucking overrated anyway. Who wants to see Dakota Fanning dancing on a banquette?"

Chase sidles up and reaches for vodka.

"Excuse me, sweetheart," Schuyler says. "We have a mission here, to kick this rum. No one gets a drink until this bottle is emptied, understood?"

Chase takes a pull. "Christ, that's lighter fluid." He coughs and passes it to Laine.

"Well done, Chase. Lainer, your turn."

"Schuyler, I can't. That shit is so gross."

"You know what? I bet you can. Chase, will you come with me for a little ciggy break?"

When Chase complies Schuyler turns back to Heather and mouths something, winks.

Laine watches Schuyler whisper in his ear and grab his hand up the staircase to the second-floor balcony. Laine's face flushes. Meanwhile, Heather has gone to the fridge.

"Lainer," she says. "Have you ever had a Jell-O shot? So good. Try one."

Laine has one. And she has another. And then Heather kindly makes her a White Russian.

"I can be, like, your own personal bartender!" Heather says.

Laine tries to thank her but it takes a minute.

Ten minutes into some quarters game and Laine has yet to figure out the rules or who she's playing with. Someone tips beer for her, and it pours out the side of her mouth.

She spills on her dress and laughs. "Oh my God. Jesus. Did I do that?"

Then she's in the bathroom, asking girls if she can try their lipstick.

"Please, please, please, pretty please?" she says.

On a bed in a room, she sits but keeps sliding off the edge. She's telling this guy about the divorce. "Are your parents, like, together, or are they divorced? Or what?" she asks, then laughs. "I *knewwww* my mom was going to divorce my dad. He was just like, *Oh, life's a dream, let's just have fun,* and my mom was like, *Straighten up! Get it together, everybody!* And it was me, I coulda tole everyone involved what was about to happen, but I didn't. So it fell apart."

Where's the guy she was talking to? "Where he go?" She has a sudden flash of self-awareness. "Did I *bore* him?" She giggles. "I migh' be drunk."

Another guy rolls his eyes at the rest of the room and turns back to her. "No shit, huh? Because I thought those field hockey stories you were telling were really poignant."

"Oh! Field hickey. The final game when I collapse was cuh-*razy*. I mean, can you 'magine? I mean, have you ever just, like, fainted, you know? It's *scary*."

From the balcony, Schuyler yells, "Jesus, Laine. I never heard you talk so much in your life. Someone get that bitch a line and straighten her ass up."

Someone pinches her left nostril and holds a clump of powder on a key under the right. "Snort," the person commands, and she does.

A long hallway, a carpet. Elevator doors.

She sees another girl, and goes up to her. No, it's a mirror. Narcissus flowers on an end table under the mirror. Herself in the reflection. Green velvet off one shoulder. Touches the flower, what is it? She already forgot—oh, it's a flower. Her face, something about it. The inside of her nostrils lined with red silk like a coat.

Here's her house! She tries to open the door, tries to open the door. *Uh-oh*, deep in her belly she knows this is wrong. She moves away from that door, moves away, stumbling, what's on her feet? *High heels*. She kicks them off, leaves them. Presses elevator button. A man in a silk robe looks out of the other door, he seems angry. She steps into the elevator, hand over her mouth. *Is he mad at me?* She presses a button.

Chase wakes on the bathroom floor, tiles cool against hot cheek. He vaguely recalls a self-induced vomiting period after sharing a bowl with Greg.

He opens the door to find Diego and two girls sharing cigarettes and calling around for X. "My friend Chase, you look a little green."

"No shit, Diego. Where is everyone?"

"I think Schuyler passed out in the main bedroom, which I am sure interests you. The rest of your team of flunkies are in the other bedroom."

"Cool. Can I bum a smoke?"

The hotel room reeks of stale cigarettes, cheap booze, and him. He needs air. Chase presses ROOF on the elevator menu. The wind hits his face hard and he steps back to light the Dunhill in the elevator. The deck is cleared for winter. The celebrities, socialites, pretenders, and impostors have all vanished to other distinguished private rooms throughout the city or maybe to Palm Beach or L.A.

Chase pushes past a few naked wooden couches and turns the corner. He sucks in slowly and watches the lights of uptown glisten as flurries fall. He laughs to himself. *Who needs stars in New York?* He keeps walking when it hits him: something there, on the ground, a handbag. He sees the footprints by the bag. Right next to the ledge.

Cigarette between his teeth, he looks through the bag, already somehow knowing what he will find. Laine's mittens, her Carmex, her ID. Chase can't breathe. This is where the footprints seem to end, so he forces himself to look over. *No no no no no,* his mind says. He can't think anything else. But it's a far way down, and the clutter down there, he can't see anything, he doesn't know, he's not sure what to look for, he's scared.

Noah and Nikki have crawled into a bed in one of the rooms. Parker, Gabriel, and Greg are wrapped in one blanket on that floor. They locked the door since the room's already a sardine can. Noah clutches Nikki, but fifteen minutes have passed and his breathing has gone from irregular to rhythmic.

"After all your big talk, Noah, I at least expected an attempt. It would have been fun rejecting you," Nikki whispers.

"I know. I'm such a pussy, but if I open my eyes right now I may just yak, so consider yourself lucky."

"Cute."

Chase raps on the door: "Open it; it's me. Hurry up."

Greg peeks out, eyes red. "What the fuck? Sleep with Schuyler."

"No. This is serious for fuck's sake, open the goddamn door. Get *up.*"

Nikki jumps out of bed. "Where's Laine?"

Chase stares at her. "I'm not sure, Nik. We got to look."

Chase offers to go downstairs, and braces himself. Greg

and Gabriel set out to search each floor. Parker starts knocking on the doors in the suite, looking like a sick fairy in her dress to all the addled people. Nikki decides to check the roof again.

The elevator door opens to drifting snow, gentle and sweet. Nikki sees the footprints, and the place where Chase picked up the bag. She moves in the big silence around the roof, making sure.

Laine's body is slumped on a bench. Her lips pale, green velvet drooping off both shoulders. A smudge of blood in her nose. Bare feet.

"Ohmygod, oh Jesus fucking Christ," Nikki whispers, pulling Laine to her. Nikki takes her coat from her shoulders and puts it around Laine. She picks up Laine's feet and cradles them in her lap, rubs them. "Laine, it's Nik. Laine."

Laine opens her eyes, looks at Nikki, and starts to cry. "I want to go home," she says.

Grand Central at 5 A.M. The clock gleams the time to all the drifters loitering on the marble floor. The gold ceiling flickers like heaven.

They were kicked out of two cabs when Laine said she had to puke. In a Bangladeshi accent, the first guy kept asking, "She be all right?"

"No," Nikki said, exasperated. "She said she's going to puke, pull over."

Neither taxi would wait, speeding away in the snow. The girls finally made it here, and now head straight to the ladies' room. Nik holds Laine's hair back as a fat blonde in uniform with prison tattoos on her forearm leans on her mop stick and glumly watches.

"Can I help you?" Nikki finally asks the woman.

Laine is wiping her mouth with toilet paper when their train to Greenwich is called.

"Okay, baby. You feel up to this?" Nikki asks.

Laine nods, sobered up now, just sick.

They step gingerly onto the bright train. Laine's wearing leopard-print slippers Nikki found at the hotel. Nikki helps her into a seat, and Laine slumps against the cool window. When they finally pull out of the tunnel, the world is turning pale at the edges. It's no longer night.

Nikki thinks Laine is sleeping, but then she says something. Nikki doesn't catch it, asks her to repeat it. With eyes still closed, Laine says, "I have to tell you something."

18

The Old Greenwich station's stone trestle will be dusted with blue dawn light. Polly will shiver in a black coat, watching the train roll up, peering into its dirty windows for her daughter. She pinches her lips when the two girls step down. She will formally introduce herself to Nikki as if they're at a cocktail party, and then look into Laine's eyes. Laine will look back. An infinity of communication, leaving tracers of light.

That morning will be hard. They'll enter the enormous house, whose rooms ring with silence. Nikki will not and cannot speak to Laine. Besides, she'll have said enough on the train, maybe too much, or with too much venom. Instead she will take a bath in a claw-footed tub on the third floor. Read a waterlogged *New Yorker* without processing the words. Each time the water cools, she'll use her foot to turn the hot faucet.

An hour later, she'll find the kitchen where Polly gets her cereal, after Nikki refuses insistent offers of anything more substantial. She won't want much from this family right now. While Nikki eats, Polly will answer the phone.

"Hello, Dean Talliworth, it's Polly Breck."

Nikki will be able to piece together the conversation from Polly's responses. *Laine failed three exams. Miss Hartford advised a break, for health reasons. And on top of that, the 60 Thompson incident had already reached the Headmaster and the board. They believe Laine should take some time off, perhaps all of next semester, before returning to Wellington, if returning was, in the end, what seemed right for her.*

That cold afternoon, wind whipping around the house, Laine will be in Philip's office. Nikki can watch TV on a cracked leather chair in the library. She'll believe Laine must be getting her ass nailed. *Good.* Snow rushes down from the sky in its slow way, burying the gardens outside the window.

But when Laine emerges, eyes red, Philip's arm will be around her, her body slumped without reservation into his. He squeezes her shoulders, whispers something to make her smile even though her eyes still glisten.

Polly worriedly turns to Nikki, who will stand up, cashmere blanket in hand. "Shall we call your father then, Nicole, to get you home, you poor thing? We'll gladly get you a car."

Laine will look at her mom. In a voice raw from crying she'll say, "Can she stay? Please?"

And then she'll face Nikki with an exalted, beautiful, demented look—a look Nikki will take years to understand. "Things have kind of fallen apart, Nikki."

A couple days later, the sky after the giant snowfall will be a sweet, bluebird blue, the clouds chubby and evolving like clouds borrowed from a children's book. Christine and Maggie will tag along after Nikki and Laine, snow boots breaking the crust and crashing through with each footfall. All four girls grin in the glare of so much white.

"Are we there?" Maggie will pant, her cheeks red and nose slick.

Laine will pick her up in her yellow pom-pom hat and red parka with last year's ski tags on it. "Yes, Miss Mags, we're almost there."

And when they do get to the top, they'll be alone, the first kids out today, the first footprints up Merrimac Hill. Chris and Mags will set up their sled together, Maggie ahead of her sister, their legs like *V*s, boots tucked in at the nose of the sleigh. They'll squeal and giggle as Nik and Laine push them to the edge, then they will be silent as they launch, rushing through snow shine.

But Laine and Nikki will not follow, and instead lie down as if their sleds were beds. The hotel, the rum, the train—these things will seem decades behind them in some ways, and never-ending in others. Nikki still won't know what to think, and it will be a while before she does. The landscape will twinkle with infinitesimal rainbows, and although they laugh at first to be lying like this outside in the snow, they will find themselves lulled, and they will imagine themselves floating—

Suspended above these blue-white hills, the pure and untracked mounds, above Greenwich itself and its iced spires and movie theater marquees and estates and parking lots and pine trees, above themselves. Nikki thinks of something Grant said: *You guys are at that age when you're becoming who you will eventually be at the speed of light.* Below them, the world dazzles.

Later they will all trudge home, bearing the smell of wet wool, with minor headaches from squinting all morning. They will strip off jackets, and lay scarves, mittens, hats, and socks on the antique radiator in the mudroom. The balls of ice will slowly melt, and the wool will slowly dry. Polly will make them hot chocolate.

TEASER TK